Welcome to Suite 4B!

Join Andie, Jina, Mary Beth, and Lauren for more fun at the Riding Academy!

And coming soon:

Mary Beth stood frozen in the middle of the room. Panic began to crawl up her insides.

She thought back to her conversation with Stephanie. Lauren had left her sister still feeling really upset. Had she gone to some secret place where she could cry alone, even though she knew it meant breaking Foxhall rules?

No, Mary Beth told herself. Lauren was too level-headed. Or was she? Had all the craziness lately pushed her into doing something dumb?

If so, then it was all Mary Beth's fault.

Turning, Mary Beth raced from Mill Hall. She had to find Lauren!

Trouble at Foxhall

by Alison Hart

BULLSEYE BOOKS

Random House New York

Mary Beth Finney tossed her auburn hair, pawed the dorm room floor with one fist, and whinnied. "How's that?" she asked her roommates.

"All wrong," Andie Perez complained. "If you're going to be Ginger from *Black Beauty*, you have to look nastier. She'd been really badly treated by her previous owner, remember?"

"Oh." Mary Beth frowned. She'd never played a horse before, so she wasn't quite sure how to act.

Mary Beth was kneeling on all fours in the middle of the dorm room floor. Lauren Remick and Jina Williams, her other two roommates at Foxhall Academy, a girls' boarding school in

Maryland, sat cross-legged on their beds. They were looking at a copy of *Black Beauty's Hints*, the play they'd written for their sixth grade English class.

"It's not like Mary Beth can pin her ears back like a real horse," Lauren pointed out. She was wearing her own long blond hair in a bushy ponytail so she would look more like a horse, too.

Andie paced between two of the beds, finally stopping in front of Mary Beth. "Maybe she needs to scowl or something."

"Horses don't scowl," Jina said. Since it was after dinner, she was already dressed in a comfortable flannel nightie, her thick black hair pulled back in a Scrunchie.

Mary Beth groaned in annoyance. She was tired of kneeling on the hard floor, pretending to be a horse. Besides, she had tons of math problems to finish for tomorrow's class and a lab report due in science. "How about if I do this?" she suggested. Stretching her neck, she grabbed Andie's pant leg with her teeth, squealed, then bit down hard.

"Ow!" Andie swatted Mary Beth's head with her script. "That hurt, Finney!"

Mary Beth collapsed on the floor, laughing.

Lauren burst out giggling, too, and Jina muffled a snicker behind her script.

"Not funny, guys," Andie huffed.

"Sorry, Andie," Mary Beth said, pushing herself up to a sitting position. "I was just trying to be Ginger." But inside, she knew that Andie wouldn't find anything funny tonight.

Andie was still super-upset. All of them were. They'd worked like crazy the whole week, earning money to help Andie buy her Magic. Then, yesterday, Dean Wilkes had told them it was against Foxhall rules to take money from other students. Andie had had to give all their hard-earned money back. Now she was worried she'd never get Magic.

Without a word, Andie flopped backward on her bed and stared gloomily at the ceiling.

"So, where's our Merrylegs? I mean, Tiffany?" Mary Beth asked, trying to change the subject.

"Her parents took her out to dinner," Lauren said.

Tiffany Dubray was another sixth-grader working on the *Black Beauty* project. Since the roommates had been busy doing chores all last week to earn money, Tiffany had ended up writing most of the script.

Jina held up the stapled pages. "Well, I hate to say it, but this play stinks."

"I agree," Lauren said. "*Black Beauty's Hints* sounds like makeover advice or something. 'Always brush out my tail with a soft brush so the ends don't split,'" she read. "'Polish my hooves until they gleam.'"

"Maybe we should send the tips to *Teen* magazine," Mary Beth suggested. "I'm sure some of the girls that read those articles look like horses."

All the roommates, even Andie, had to grin.

"Mary Beth! Telephone!" someone yelled from the outside hall.

Mary Beth scrambled to her feet. "Must be my parents," she said, heading for the door. "They always call Sunday nights."

"Hurry back," Lauren called after her. "We need to fix up this play or Mrs. James will give us a big fat D on Wednesday."

"This play is so lame, she might just give us an E," Mary Beth heard Andie grumble as she started down the hall. It was busy with girls arriving back at Foxhall from the weekend away.

Mary Beth envied the returning students. She would have loved a weekend home. It was

4

too bad Cedarville was so far away. She really liked Foxhall, but the past week at school had been really long. And she missed her family a lot.

"Mom!" she said happily when she picked up the receiver.

"Mom?" a guy's voice on the other end repeated.

Mary Beth felt herself flush. It was Tommy Isaacson, her sort-of boyfriend from the Manchester School.

"Do I sound like your mother?" Tommy joked.

"Sorry," Mary Beth replied. "My parents usually call around now. How are you doing?" Mary Beth hadn't seen Tommy since the interschool horse show last weekend.

"Great. I was thinking of you guys, though. Remember jumping in the hotel pool and ganging up on that girl, Jennifer Schwartz?" He laughed. "That was a cool idea Lauren came up with."

"Yeah, real cool," Mary Beth said flatly. She couldn't believe it. She'd only been on the phone with Tommy a minute and already he'd mentioned Lauren!

"I just wanted to say good-bye before you

5

left for Thanksgiving break," Tommy continued. "Would you give me your home phone number?"

Mary Beth's heart started to pound. "Sure. I mean, if you really want to call me at home..."

"No," Tommy said, "I asked for your number so I can call and order pizzas."

Mary Beth blushed again. Why did she always say such dumb things to guys? "School lets out Friday," she told Tommy. "I'll be home until the Friday after Thanksgiving. Then we're all going to Jina's."

"That's great. Is Lauren going, too?"

Mary Beth pressed her lips together. Why did he want to know about Lauren?

She twisted the phone cord around her wrist. "Uh, yeah. We're going to sleep over Friday night, then go foxhunting on Saturday."

"Foxhunting! Double cool. Are you going to jump?"

Mary Beth shook her head, even though she knew Tommy couldn't see her. "No way. I'm going to hill-top or whatever it's called."

"That'll be fun."

"I guess." There was an awkward silence. Mary Beth wondered if other girls knew what to say to guys they really liked. *Lauren always knows the right stuff to talk about*, she thought darkly.

"Well, are you going to tell me your phone number?" Tommy asked finally.

"All right." Mary Beth grinned as she gave it to him. *Forget about Lauren*, she told herself. *You're the one Tommy wants to call over the holiday. He must really like you.*

"So how did Lauren do on that math test she was all worried about?" Tommy asked.

Lauren again! Mary Beth fumed silently. She bit her lip hard, trying not to get mad. Tommy and Lauren were just friends—even though Lauren *had* spent a lot of time with him at last weekend's horse show.

A lot more time than you did, Mary Beth reminded herself.

"I know she was really studying hard," Tommy continued.

That did it. Mary Beth let out her breath in a loud burst. "Since you're so interested, why don't you just ask her yourself?" she snapped. "I'll go get her." She dropped the receiver so abruptly, it clonked against the wall.

Fists tight at her sides, Mary Beth pushed rudely past several girls who were dragging suitcases down the hall. When she reached the

7

partly open door to suite 4B, she halted. Lauren was still sitting next to Jina on the bed, studying the play. Her ponytail hung over one shoulder, and she wore her fuzzy puppy-head slippers and pink-flowered bathrobe.

Mary Beth glanced down at her own baggy sweatpants and a Foxhall Academy sweatshirt. *No fair*, she thought. *Lauren looks cute no matter what she wears.*

"Tommy's on the phone," she announced through clenched teeth. "He wants to know how you did on your math test."

Lauren looked up. "Tell him it's tomorrow."

"No, *you* tell him," Mary Beth declared, her anger suddenly exploding. "*You're* the one he wants to talk to, Miss Perfect Lauren Remick. Not me!"

2

Mary Beth stomped past Lauren into the suite. Plucking her bath bucket off the top of her dresser, she marched into the bathroom, slamming the door behind her.

Feeling miserable, she stared at her image in the mirror. Her auburn hair was looped behind her ears, making them stick out more than ever, and her cheeks were blotchy from yelling.

Tears formed in her eyes. She couldn't believe the way she'd just exploded at Lauren. Her roommate hadn't done anything. So what was the problem?

It *had* been a crazy week, and Mary Beth had gotten behind in her schoolwork. Tommy *had* talked about Lauren a lot. But that was no excuse.

"You're just homesick, Finney," Mary Beth told the mirror. It was true. She missed Benji, Reed, Tammy, Dogums, and her mom and dad—big-time.

She'd been at Foxhall for almost three months now, with only one visit from her family. That was the longest she'd been away from them in all her life.

But why are you taking it out on Lauren? Mary Beth asked herself as she bent to splash cold water on her face. It wasn't fair to her friend.

Straightening, she dried her face on her towel. *Maybe I am jealous of her*, Mary Beth thought as she combed her hair. Lauren always seemed so perfect. She was everything Mary Beth wasn't—a good rider, cute, petite, bubbly, and confident.

Mary Beth sighed and tucked her comb back into her bath bucket. *Not true.* She knew Lauren had her own problems, especially in math. And that was one thing Mary Beth was definitely good at.

She took a deep breath and picked up her bath bucket. She knew she had to go out and apologize. No one needed another week like the last one.

When she opened the bathroom door, Lauren glanced up at her, a puzzled expression on her face. She was sitting on the edge of her bed—alone.

Avoiding Lauren's eyes, Mary Beth went over to her dresser and set her bath bucket carefully on top. She knew she had to say something. She just wasn't sure what.

"So, where are Jina and Andie?" she asked finally, her back to Lauren as she pulled a crumpled nightshirt from the corner of the tall wardrobe the girls shared.

"They went to the common room to make popcorn," Lauren said. "We weren't getting anywhere with this stupid play."

Mary Beth heard pages rustle. She shut the wardrobe door, then turned to face Lauren.

"I'm sorry I yelled at you," she said, looking down at the wadded-up nightie.

Lauren didn't say anything right away. Mary Beth lifted her chin. Her roommate was ripping off the corners of the pages and dropping them on the floor.

"I'm sorry, too," she said. "And Tommy was totally confused. He couldn't figure out why you just cut him off like that."

Mary Beth folded and unfolded her nightshirt. "I'm not sure I know, either," she mumbled.

"You know I don't like Tommy as a boyfriend," Lauren added. "I think he's really nice and all, but he's not my type."

"Too young?" Mary Beth quipped. Lauren had had a huge crush on Todd Jenkins, Jina's trainer, for ages.

"Yeah." Lauren tried to laugh, but Mary Beth could tell it was forced.

Just then, Andie and Jina burst into the room, carrying puffed-up bags of microwave popcorn. "Popcorn's ready!" Andie announced.

"Great!" Mary Beth said eagerly, glad her roommates had interrupted the awkward conversation.

While Jina passed out paper towels, Mary Beth peeked over at Lauren. She was still shredding the play, a hill of paper forming at her feet.

Mary Beth wanted to kick herself. But she knew it was too late. Her outburst had really hurt Lauren's feelings.

Sadness washed over her. Would Lauren forgive her? Mary Beth hoped so. She didn't want to lose her best friend at Foxhall.

*   *   *

12

"Did you hear the big news?" Andie asked excitedly at lunch the next day.

"No, what?" Mary Beth answered as she speared a tomato to put on top of her ham, cheese, bologna, lettuce, and onion piled on a roll. Monday was cold-cuts day in the Foxhall cafeteria, and Mary Beth loved building huge multidecker sandwiches.

Andie picked up her tray. "Pete Previtti delivered a new school horse this morning."

"Really?" Mary Beth continued to concentrate on her growing sandwich. Maybe it needed a little mustard.

"Yeah. I saw Katherine before lunch. She said the new mare is real cute." Craning her neck, Andie looked around the cafeteria. "Hey, there's Jina. She's got a table already. Meet you there."

"Right." Mary Beth scooped a handful of chips from a huge bowl, then headed across the cafeteria to the spot where Jina sat with Andie and two other girls. Since lunches were informal, the girls could sit anywhere they wanted.

"The new horse is adorable," Shandra Thomas, a sixth-grader, was saying to Jina, Andie, and Heidi Olson. Shandra and Heidi

13

were beginning riders like Mary Beth. "She's a palomino. That's what Mrs. Caufield said, anyway."

"You saw the new horse already?" Jina asked.

Mary Beth set down her tray, then sat next to Shandra, who was nodding vigorously.

"Yep." Shandra took a sip of her fruit punch. "This morning I had to go to the barn and finish that quiz we took on caring for horses in cold weather. Pete was just unloading her."

Mary Beth opened her carton of milk. "So, what's a palomino?"

Heidi Olson, who was sitting on Mary Beth's left, turned to look at her. "You don't know what a palomino is?" she asked in disbelief.

"Well, excu-u-use me," Mary Beth shot back. Even though Heidi was a beginning rider, too, she was already doing a smooth canter and had passed all her written tests with flying colors. And sometimes, Mary Beth thought darkly, she liked to flaunt it.

Andie laughed so hard that juice began to spurt from her mouth.

"Gross, Andie," Jina said, scooting her chair away from her.

Andie slapped her palm over her mouth. "Sorry. But you have to admit, Finney here can be pretty dumb."

"I don't know what a palomino is either," Shandra admitted. Shandra lived in Baltimore. Before coming to Foxhall, she had never seen a horse except on TV.

"A palomino is the color of a horse that's golden with a whitish mane and tail," Jina told Mary Beth and Shandra. "And it's a breed, too. Like a Thoroughbred."

"Oh." Mary Beth nodded as if she understood perfectly, even though she really didn't. How could a breed be a color?

Not that she cared about a new horse. She and Dangerous Dan were getting along okay. They'd even won two ribbons at the last horse show. So maybe his hooves were too big and his neck was too fat. Maybe she did have to show him the crop whenever he got poky, but at least he wasn't half wild like Magic or lame like Jina's horse, Superstar.

Using both hands, Mary Beth picked up her sandwich. Tomato and bologna immediately slid out the sides.

"Where's Lauren?" she asked Andie, taking a huge bite.

15

Andie shrugged. "How should I know? I'm not her mother."

While she chewed, Mary Beth scanned the cafeteria. There was no sign of their roommate. This morning, Lauren had left early, saying she had to get to math class. It had been the first time in ages that Mary Beth hadn't walked with her to breakfast.

Later, in English class, Lauren had been really quiet. *She's still mad at me,* Mary Beth thought sadly, a lump forming in her throat. Or was that just a piece of roll? She coughed it up, then swallowed hard. She'd have to think of some way to make things okay again.

"There's Lauren." Jina pointed to the entrance.

Lauren was just coming in behind a group of older girls. Her arms were full of books. Her usually rosy cheeks were pale, and wisps of blond hair had escaped from her braid.

"Man, she looks pooped," Andie said. "That math test must have been a killer."

The math test! Mary Beth dropped her sandwich. That's why Lauren had been so worried all morning. It wasn't because Mary Beth had yelled at her last night.

Lauren came over to the table and dropped

16

her books between Jina and Andie. "Hi, guys," she said wearily.

"How'd it go?" Mary Beth asked.

Lauren shrugged. "Who knows? I tried. My tutor tried. Mrs. Jacquin tried." She sighed. "I did all right on some parts, I think. But when it came to adding fractions with unlike denominators, it was like reading Spanish or something."

Adding fractions? Mary Beth wrinkled her nose. She couldn't believe Lauren was still doing something that easy.

"Then you should have let me help," Andie said. "I know Spanish." She patted the seat next to her. "Sit down. I'll get you some juice."

Mary Beth, Lauren, and Jina all stared at Andie in surprise. Andie wasn't usually that nice.

Andie jumped up. "Hey, don't look at me like I'm some kind of weirdo. I have to get up anyway and get myself a refill." Flipping her thick hair behind her shoulders, she strode off.

Jina frowned. "That's the first real sign of life Andie's shown since Saturday. You don't think she's cooking up another scheme to buy Magic, do you?"

Lauren dropped into the chair and rested

her head on her folded arms. "I hope not. I think that's what blew it for me. All last week I should have been concentrating on math instead of cleaning bathrooms and making beds to raise money for Magic."

Mary Beth nodded in agreement. "We all should have been studying. Look how that *Black Beauty* play turned out."

"After we all worked on it last night, it's not that bad," Jina said. "Is it?" she asked hesitantly when Mary Beth and Lauren didn't answer.

Mary Beth pushed back her chair. "'Oh, Beauty, oh, Beauty,'" she recited dramatically, her hand pressed to her chest. Heidi and Shandra stopped talking to stare at her. "'You saved your mistress's life! Yes, you saved her life!'"

"Is your play supposed to be a comedy?" Shandra asked.

Mary Beth, Jina, and Lauren burst out laughing.

"No. Mary Beth's just making it sound funny," Lauren said, still giggling. Mary Beth grinned happily, glad that Lauren didn't seem mad at her anymore.

"What's so funny?" Andie demanded when she returned to the table with two drinks.

"Nothing," Mary Beth said. Then she caught Lauren's eye, and the two of them cracked up all over again.

Not because *Black Beauty's Hints* was so hilarious, Mary Beth decided. She just felt happy.

Lauren was still her friend.

3

"Why is your blanket so huge, Dan?" Mary Beth puffed later that afternoon as she tugged and pulled on her school horse's green quilted blanket. She'd unbuckled it and folded it in thirds. Now she was trying to slide it off his broad back.

"I know, I know," she grumbled. "It's because *you're* so huge."

With a grunt, Mary Beth yanked hard. The blanket slid suddenly into her arms, throwing her off balance, and she staggered backward. A surcingle flew in the air, its metal buckle popping her in the cheek.

"Ow!" Mary Beth fell back against the wall, hitting the wood slats with a loud whack.

Dan turned to stare at her lazily, one brow cocked. Then he snorted out a wad of gook

20

and continued to pick around in his straw for any stray stalks of hay.

Mary Beth let out her own breath. "Thanks for the help, you big clod."

Hoisting the blanket in her arms, she half carried, half dragged it to Dan's stall door. Since the top half was open, she could drape it over the bottom. *If* she could get it up that high.

"Mary Beth, are you in there?" someone called.

"Yes, I'm in here," Mary Beth panted as she lifted up the blanket.

Andie stood in the aisle, staring into the stall. She was dressed in a warm coat and chaps zipped over her jeans. Her riding helmet was perched on her head, its strap dangling.

"Oh, it *is* you, Finney," Andie said in fake surprise. "I thought it was a horse blanket that had come alive!" She screamed in mock horror.

"Ha, ha." Mary Beth glared at her roommate. "You wouldn't think it was so funny if *your* horse's blanket was the size of a king-size bedspread."

Andie's smile instantly died. "I don't have a horse, remember? Magic's not mine." Grabbing the end of the blanket, she helped Mary

Beth pull it halfway over the door. "But I'm working on it."

Mary Beth touched the spot beneath her eye where the buckle had whacked her. It really hurt.

"Do I have a bruise?" She leaned over the stall door, her cheek tilted toward Andie.

Andie narrowed her eyes, studying the spot where Mary Beth was pointing. "Nope. Only a million freckles and a big zit."

"Gee, thanks a lot." Mary Beth picked a brush out of Dan's grooming kit. "So why aren't you getting Magic ready for your lesson? You're going to be late."

Turning, she started to brush Dan. At least the big blanket had kept him clean. Usually, when he was turned out in the pasture during the day, he rolled in the muddiest spot he could find.

"I'm not riding Magic today," Andie said, sounding dejected. "Caufield wants me to give him a break. I'm supposed to ride Ranger."

"What's so bad about that?"

Andie sighed. "Because now that I don't have the money to buy Magic, I'm afraid Caufield is going to give him to other girls to ride."

"Maybe she just wants you to learn about other horses."

Andie laid her arms on the top of the blanket and rested her chin on them. "Only I don't want to learn about other horses."

Mary Beth sighed and kept brushing. She wished Andie would go away. Her gloomy roommate was getting to be a drag.

"So, have you seen the new horse yet?" Andie asked a few minutes later.

Mary Beth shook her head. "Nope." Dust from Dan's flank flew in the air, making her sneeze. Standing on tiptoe, she tried to reach his back.

"Shandra was right. She really is cute. Her name is Sunset's Fawn."

Mary Beth snorted. "What a sissy name." She bent to whisk away some manure clinging to Dan's fetlock hairs.

"Yeah, well, I guess I'd better go tack up Ranger," Andie said unenthusiastically. "See you."

"See you." Mary Beth dropped the brush back in the grooming kit and hunted for her hoof pick. Cleaning out Dan's hooves was always a challenge. Even though he stood patiently as she held and picked out each hoof, it was like holding up a boulder.

When Mary Beth finally finished, sweat was dribbling down her forehead. Tiredly, she wiped it off with her coat sleeve. Then, checking her watch, she realized that if she didn't hurry, she'd be late for her lesson. Not that she wasn't used to being late. Dan was so big, he always took forever to groom.

Fifteen minutes later, she finally had Dan tacked up. "Time for our lesson," Mary Beth told him as she opened the bottom stall door and stepped into the aisle. A cold November wind whipped around the corner of the barn, instantly freezing her ears.

She shivered. At least her lesson would be indoors today.

She turned back to Dan. "Coming?" The big horse hadn't budged. Mary Beth tugged on the reins. "This is no time for a strike," she told him. "We canter again today." *Ugh.*

Dan yawned, flashing his huge teeth. Mary Beth quit tugging on the reins. She knew exactly how he felt. She hated to canter, too. The two of them galumphed up the side of the arena like a monkey on an elephant.

Mary Beth's shoulders drooped. Sometimes she wondered why she stuck with riding anyway. If she'd signed up for dance at the beginning of school, as she'd planned, she'd be in a warm gym right now, practicing graceful port de bras and pirouettes.

But if you'd taken dance, you'd still be scared to death of horses, Mary Beth reminded herself. At least she'd gotten over that. Almost.

"Please, Dan?" she begged, stepping back into the stall. "I promise I'll rub you down extra hard afterward and"—she lowered her voice to a whisper—"I'll bring you a big shiny apple tomorrow."

Dan flapped his rubbery lips, then shuffled slowly toward the open door. Mary Beth gave him a pat. "Attaboy. You can do it. One more step and we're out the door."

Finally, Mary Beth got the huge horse from the stall to the courtyard in front of the stable. It was empty.

Late again. Quickly, she led Dan down the drive to the indoor arena. By the time she reached the entrance, she saw that the other beginning riders—Shandra, Heidi, and Becky, a new student—were trotting small circles. In the middle of the ring, the stable manager, Dorothy Germaine, hollered instructions in her gravelly voice.

Mary Beth halted in the entryway, not sure what to do. Just then, Jina hurried up to her. She wasn't wearing her riding clothes, and she held a halter and longe line in her hand.

"Why aren't you riding?" Mary Beth asked in surprise.

"Mrs. Caufield didn't have a horse for me," Jina explained. "So she asked me to work with you today on some balance exercises."

"Just me?" When Jina glanced awkwardly away, Mary Beth understood what was going on.

Her cheeks grew hot. "Oh, I get it. You're working with the klutz of the group."

Jina's gaze dropped to her toes. "No. I'll probably work with all the beginning riders. Just not today."

"Oh, sure you will," Mary Beth said sarcastically. She was clutching the reins so tightly her fingers hurt. Then she gave up. She shouldn't take out her frustrations on Jina. It wasn't her roommate's fault she was a lousy rider.

"Okay, so what are these great exercises that will make me an Olympic champion?"

"Well, first we need to—" Jina began. Just then, a horse and rider came up behind Dan, who was still blocking the entrance.

"Excuse me!" the rider called out.

Mary Beth turned. It was Katherine Parks, the dressage instructor. Usually she was giving lessons at this time in the afternoon, so Mary Beth was surprised to see her on a horse.

Clucking to Dan, Mary Beth led him toward the side of the arena. He went with her reluctantly, stopping dead when she slowed to see if Jina was following them.

"Dan, come on." She pulled sharply on the reins, catching him in the mouth with the bit. Instantly, he stepped forward, crunching down on her toe.

"Ow!" Mary Beth screeched, jerking her foot out from under his hoof. She stooped to survey the damage. The end of her boot was squashed flat, but luckily his hoof had only caught the nail of her big toe.

She wiggled it, grimacing in pain.

"Are you all right?" Jina asked, coming up.

Mary Beth threw up her hands in exasperation. "Oh, sure. Every day it's another embarrassing moment. Dan and I are like a comedy team."

Jina just smiled.

"Sometimes I think I could do better if I had a different horse," Mary Beth said with a sigh. "One that wasn't such a *clod*." She directed the last word at Dan, but his eyelids were already drooping as he tried to catch a quick nap.

"Maybe Mrs. Caufield will let you ride the new horse," Jina said, pointing toward the ring.

Mary Beth spun around. Katherine was trotting past them on Sunset's Fawn. The mare was small—about fifteen hands—with a graceful arched neck, tiny hooves, and a sweet face.

And she was the most beautiful color Mary Beth had ever seen. Her coat shone like a Christmas star and her white mane and tail flowed soft and full.

"Wow!" Mary Beth breathed. "She's—she's *beautiful*."

Jina nodded in agreement. "Katherine's trying her out first, but I heard she's so well trained that even beginners can ride her."

"Where did she come from?" Mary Beth asked. "Why would someone sell such a gorgeous animal?"

"Katherine said that Fawn belonged to a girl who rode her in Pony Club. Now she's going away to study overseas or something, so she donated her to the school."

"Did you say even a beginner could ride her?" Mary Beth said eagerly.

"Yup."

Mary Beth drew in her breath as Katherine trotted the palomino in a figure eight. The mare moved softly, like a ballet dancer performing a delicate movement.

Mary Beth couldn't believe it. Sunset's Fawn looked like a dream come true. "Do you think there's a chance *I* could ride her?" she asked Jina.

Jina shrugged. "It wouldn't hurt to ask, I guess."

Just then, Dan bumped against Mary Beth's back, trying to scratch his forehead. His movement caught her by surprise, and when he pushed her hard with his nose, the force sent her flying. Arms outstretched, she plowed headfirst into the sand and sawdust of the arena floor.

Coughing and gagging, she pushed herself up on her hands and knees. Her unstrapped helmet fell to the ground. She could hear the other riders laughing at her.

"That does it," Mary Beth sputtered as she spit out a wad of sawdust. *The ultimate humiliation. Dan and I are through.*

Tomorrow she would convince Mrs. Caufield to assign Sunset's Fawn to her. It was time she, Mary Beth Finney, got to ride a dream horse.

4

"Are you all right, Mary Beth?" Jina choked out. She was obviously trying to hold back her laughter.

Mary Beth sat back on her heels and wiped the dirt from her face. Then, picking up her helmet, she rose to her feet.

"I'm fine," she announced, slapping the dirt from her jeans. Then, turning, she scowled at Dan. He was busy scratching his head on his knee. Mary Beth's gaze swung back to Fawn. Katherine was cantering her around the arena now. The mare moved as smoothly as a cloud floating through the sky. The other beginning riders had halted their horses in the middle of the arena to watch Fawn, too.

Mary Beth bet they all wanted to ride the new horse. But she was going to beat them to it. She'd convince Mrs. Caufield that *she*, Mary Beth Finney, should be the one to ride Fawn.

Mary Beth plunked her riding helmet on her head. First, she had to show the riding instructor that she could handle a horse like Fawn.

"Okay, Jina, let's get started on those exercises," she declared. "I'm going to learn how to sit quietly in the saddle even if I have to tie myself down with rope!"

"Good, Mary Beth!" Jina praised her a few minutes later.

"Thanks!" Mary Beth said, a grin stretching across her dirty face.

Arms held straight out, she sat on Dan as he trotted in a small circle. Jina stood in the middle, holding on to the end of the longe line, which was attached to the halter Dan wore over his bridle.

Every muscle in Mary Beth's arms, back, and legs burned, but she'd actually done it. For the past few minutes, she'd trotted with no reins and no stirrups, using just her balance to keep herself secure in the saddle.

"Whoa, Dan," Jina crooned.

Mary Beth flopped forward onto her horse's

mane, exhausted. "Good boy." She patted his neck.

Jina came toward them, rolling up the longe line as she walked. "I think that trotting exercise really helped."

Mary Beth nodded. "Me too," she said. "Maybe now Mrs. Caufield will see I'm ready to ride another horse."

Jina arched a dark brow. "You're serious, aren't you?"

"Yeah. I mean, Dan's all right, but..." Grabbing a hunk of mane, Mary Beth swung her right leg over the back of the saddle and slid to the ground. "He's just so big and slow."

Jina scratched the star on Dan's forehead. "True. But he's awfully forgiving."

"What does *that* mean?" Mary Beth asked as she wiped a ribbon of sweat from her cheek. Looking up, she saw that Katherine had halted Fawn and was asking the mare to back up. Without a moment's hesitation, the palomino tucked her chin to her chest and took three steps backward.

"It means if you make a mistake, Dan doesn't care," Jina explained. "He won't run off or get nervous."

"That's for sure." Mary Beth thought back

to Halloween weekend when Tommy had been riding Lukas beside Dan and Mary Beth. Lukas had reared suddenly, causing Tommy to lose his reins. Fortunately, Dan had stayed so calm that Mary Beth had been able to grab the dangling reins before Lukas ran off.

She sighed. "I'm probably not ready for a horse that's as well trained as Fawn. I'd ruin her."

"Oh, I don't know about that," Jina said loyally. "I'll tell Mrs. Caufield how well you did today. How's that?"

Mary Beth flashed Jina a grateful smile. "That'd be super. And thanks for the help. I guess I'd better join the others for the rest of the lesson."

"And I've got to take Superstar for a walk," Jina said, unsnapping the longe line from Dan's halter. Last September, Jina's horse had bowed a tendon. Even though his leg was healing nicely, it would still be a long time before she could ride him.

Mary Beth waved good-bye, then led Dan toward the class. Katherine had halted Fawn in the middle of the arena so she could adjust the strap on her helmet.

As Mary Beth led Dan past them, she slowed. Fawn turned her head and gazed curiously at Mary Beth with her expressive dark brown eyes.

I think she likes me, too, Mary Beth thought excitedly.

Just then Katherine picked up the reins. "Walk," she crooned to Fawn. Immediately, the mare moved forward.

Mary Beth couldn't believe how giddy she felt. Now she actually knew what her roommates meant when they talked about being horse-crazy.

"Coming, Mary Beth?" Dorothy called from the circle of horses and riders.

Mary Beth snapped back to attention. Clucking to Dan, she hurried over to the other beginners. Heidi, mounted on Windsor, looked down at her. "How was your longe lesson? A little bumpy?"

"Smooth as pudding," Mary Beth replied, ignoring the smug tone in Heidi's voice.

"Listen up, ladies," Dorothy interrupted. "The Winter Indoor Schooling Circuit, otherwise known as WISC, has classes for everyone. And I do mean *everyone.* Our next show will be in January, after the Christmas break. You will all be entered in at least one schooling hack class."

Shandra raised her hand. "Uh, what's 'schooling hack' mean?"

"It means walk, trot, canter, and we don't expect you to be perfect," Dorothy answered. Everybody laughed.

Fawn and I will be perfect, Mary Beth thought when the laughter died. Looping her arm over Dan's neck, she leaned against him and stared dreamily into space.

She pictured herself riding Fawn from the arena, a blue ribbon fluttering from the golden mare's bridle. Her roommates would be in the stands, whistling and cheering. Even Mrs. Caufield would nod her head and say, "I always knew Mary Beth and Fawn would be winners."

"Hey, Mary Beth, it's time to mount up," Heidi said loudly.

Mary Beth dropped her arm from around Dan's neck. "Mount up?" She looked around in confusion. The other girls were riding their horses toward the outside arena wall.

"Right." Mary Beth hurried around to Dan's left side. Quickly, she readjusted the stirrups that had been crossed over Dan's neck for the longe lesson.

But before she could mount, Dorothy came up and put a hand on her shoulder. "Aren't you forgetting something, Ms. Finney?"

Mary Beth grimaced. Dorothy must have known she wasn't paying attention.

"Um," she stammered. "I'm not sure. I was kind of daydreaming when you were giving instructions."

Dorothy crossed her arms. The older woman's gray hair was so short, it looked like a cap. "Think about what you might be forgetting," she repeated.

Mary Beth racked her brain. She had her helmet and her crop. She'd fixed the stirrups and checked the girth. Her gaze rested on Dan's head. *The bridle! Oops.*

"I still have the halter on over the bridle," she admitted sheepishly.

"Right." Dorothy uncrossed her arms. "And with the reins secured under the throatlatch, it would be a mite hard to steer."

Mary Beth felt her cheeks flush pink. "Sorry." Quickly, she unbuckled the halter.

What a bonehead you are, Finney, she told herself as she slid the halter off Dan's head and handed it to Dorothy. If she'd ridden off with no reins, Dan probably wouldn't have noticed, but everybody else would have.

Mary Beth glanced nervously over her shoulder, wondering if anybody *had* seen her mistake. Dorothy was facing the other three girls now, shouting about heels and calves. Heidi, Shandra, and Becky were busy concentrating on improving their positions.

Mary Beth sighed in relief. Then a horrible thought occurred to her. What if Dorothy told Mrs. Caufield what she'd almost done?

The thought made her palms sweat. If that happened, Mary Beth knew the riding director would *never* assign Fawn to her.

5

"Guys, this is our last day to practice," Tiffany Dubray announced as she, Jina, Lauren, Mary Beth, and Andie trooped out of their English class Tuesday morning. "Tomorrow we have to give our play in front of the whole class!"

Mary Beth wrinkled her nose. "And boy, does it stink."

"So do you," Andie said cheerfully, pretending to sniff the air. Mary Beth, Jina, and Lauren burst out laughing.

"Get serious," Tiffany said, frowning. As usual, the leggings and sweater outfit Tiffany wore matched perfectly. Even her hair band and socks were color-coordinated. Mary Beth figured Tiffany spent hours every morning picking out her clothes—while she, Mary Beth, barely had enough time to find jeans and a turtleneck that were clean.

"I need at least a B on this stupid play or my whole grade will go down." Tiffany's voice rose in a whine.

"Tiffany's right," Jina said. "I want a decent grade, too. Let's get permission tonight to practice together during study hall."

"Sounds good to me." Lauren shifted her books in her arms and checked her watch. "You guys decide what time. I need to get to math. Mrs. Jacquin is giving our tests back today." Waving good-bye, she hurried down the hall.

"Eight o'clock," Tiffany said.

"That's fine with me," Jina said.

Andie nodded. "I really don't care. Let's just get it over with."

Mary Beth swung her backpack over her shoulder, then poked Jina with her elbow. "We'd better get to class."

After saying good-bye to Andie and Tiffany, Mary Beth and Jina walked quickly toward the Math and Science building.

"Did you ask Mrs. Caufield about riding Fawn?" Jina asked as they hurried down the sidewalk. The sun shone brightly, but the winter air was sharp.

Hunching against the cold, Mary Beth stuck her hands in the pockets of her purple jeans. The wind cut right through the sweater she was wearing, but she hated lugging a coat around when she was going from one heated building to another.

"No, I didn't have a chance. I'll ask her this afternoon." She glanced at Jina, who had pulled the hood of her jacket over her head. "I'm sort of nervous, though. What if she thinks I'm crazy?"

"Why would she think you're crazy? You're getting to be a good rider."

Mary Beth snorted. "Yeah, right." She didn't dare tell Jina about almost riding Dan with no reins.

"You are." Jina opened the door to the Math and Science building. "Trust me." Flashing an encouraging smile, she disappeared down the hall to her classroom.

Mary Beth stepped into the warm hall. It was crowded with girls rushing to class. For a few moments, she just stood there, watching the hall grow empty. Was Jina right? Had she really gotten to be a good rider?

No, she told herself. She'd done so many dumb things around horses that she'd need her fingers *and* toes to count them all.

The bell rang, loud and jangly. With a sigh, Mary Beth walked slowly into her science room. Still, she decided, she *had* improved. And if Dorothy hadn't told Mrs. Caufield about yesterday, the director might assign her Fawn. Mary Beth just had to keep her fingers crossed.

"Okay, Dan, this is it," Mary Beth said as she led the chestnut gelding across the courtyard. Lessons were over for the day. Mary Beth had been walking Dan up and down the drive, cooling him off.

She halted him in the outside aisle in front of his stall. The older barn was horseshoe-shaped, the stalls facing a grassy courtyard. An overhang protected the aisle and the stalls during bad weather.

"I'm going to ask Mrs. Caufield if I can ride Fawn," Mary Beth told Dan as she slid her hand under the blue wool cooler, which covered him from head to tail. His skin felt warm and dry.

"Not that I don't like *you*," she reassured him quickly. He tugged on the lead, eager to get back in his stall. "But maybe a break would be good—for both of us. You've got to be sick of me threatening you with that crop all the time, right?"

Just then Andie came down the aisle, leading Mr. Magic. "Talking to your horse again?" she teased, halting the handsome mahogany bay Thoroughbred next to Dan. "Maybe Dan can give you some tips for your love life. Like how to keep Lauren from stealing your dorky boyfriend."

"Oh, shut up." Mary Beth stuck her tongue out at her roommate. Andie was always making trouble, so Mary Beth had learned to ignore half of what she said. "Lauren's *not* trying to steal my boyfriend." Turning, she untied Dan's cooler.

"Well, she did call him today before riding."

Mary Beth spun around. "What?"

"Oops." Andie slapped her palm to her mouth. "Uh, I thought you knew. Well, guess I'd better get Magic back to his stall," she said quickly. She rushed down the aisle, Magic in tow.

Mary Beth, her mouth hanging open in surprise, watched her roommate hurry away. She knew from the way Andie was speeding off that her roommate hadn't been kidding. And

43

Lauren *had* called Tommy.

A flush of anger swept up Mary Beth's neck. She glanced around the barn area, wondering if Lauren had finished her lesson. She spied her walking with Jina down the opposite aisle. The two were talking together as they headed toward Mrs. Caufield's office.

"Come on," Mary Beth growled, pulling Dan into his stall. "I'm going to ask Ms. Perfect Remick why she called *my* boyfriend."

Mary Beth unhooked the lead from Dan's halter and slammed out of the stall. She was going to settle this with Lauren once and for all.

When she reached the office, she paused. Her roommates were already inside. She couldn't just burst in if Mrs. Caufield was there.

Then Mary Beth heard voices from behind the closed door of the director's office. "Fawn...super."

She leaned closer. The voice sounded like Mrs. Caufield's.

Tilting her head, Mary Beth listened.

"Watched...lessons."

That was definitely Jina's voice. Were the three of them talking about Fawn? Or was Jina

44

telling the director how well Mary Beth had ridden yesterday? Mary Beth's anger dissolved as she thought about the new horse. Maybe this would be a good time to ask Mrs. Caufield about assigning Fawn to her.

She raised her fist, ready to knock. But she froze when she heard Lauren say, "Mary Beth can't...ride Fawn."

The four words rang out loud and clear. Mary Beth drew back from the door as if she'd been burned.

At first she couldn't believe what Lauren had said. But then she knew she must have heard it right.

Her so-called friend was telling Mrs. Caufield that Mary Beth couldn't ride the new horse!

Mary Beth ran away from the office, tears spilling from her eyes.

First Tommy, now Fawn. Why was Lauren doing this to her?

She raced across the courtyard to Dan's stall, afraid that Lauren and Jina might come out and see her. Several riders cooling their horses paused to stare at her.

But Mary Beth didn't care. About anything. Her best friend had betrayed her—big-time.

Throwing open the stall door, Mary Beth rushed in, her toe catching on some blue material that was lying on the floor. She flew forward, arms outstretched, hitting Dan broadside. Just in time, she grabbed on to a hunk of his mane and kept herself from tumbling to the floor. Dan grunted but didn't budge.

"Thanks, Dan," she gasped, straightening up. With a snort, he stuck his head in the feed bucket.

Mary Beth laughed. "Oh, all right. I guess that heroic save deserves a treat." She pulled a carrot she'd saved from lunch out of her pocket and tossed it in the bucket. Then she glanced down, wondering what she'd tripped over.

Dan's cooler!

"Oh, no!" She groaned, smacking her forehead. She'd untied his cooler, then forgotten to take it off!

Smooth move, Finney. Mary Beth stooped to pick the cooler up. It had fallen in a fresh pile of manure, and then Dan had stepped on it. Mary Beth wrinkled her nose at the greenish-brown stain.

Lauren might be a traitor, she thought. But her friend—*ex-friend,* she corrected herself—was right. She, Mary Beth, wasn't ready for a horse like Fawn.

She glanced over at Dan, who was snuffling in his empty feed bucket. Then she noticed that, in her rush, she'd left the stall door wide open.

Any other horse would have spooked when she'd slammed into him, then bolted for the open door. But not good old Dan.

What had Jina called him? *Forgiving.*

Mary Beth draped the cooler over the door. Then she turned and gave Dan a big hug. "Thanks again, guy," she whispered.

But her smile soon faded. *Dan* might be forgiving. But she wasn't. She still needed to find out what was going on with Lauren.

"Hi, Mary Beth," a cheery voice greeted her.

Mary Beth jumped a foot in the air. *Lauren!*

Her roommate was standing outside the stall, staring down at Dan's cooler. "What happened?" she asked, pointing to the stain.

"Nothing!" Mary Beth snapped.

Lauren jerked back. "What's wrong with *you*?"

"Lots." Mary Beth took a stiff-legged step forward. "I heard you called Tommy."

Lauren's blue eyes widened. "Yeah. So?"

"So?" Mary Beth exclaimed. Her roommate was acting so innocent. "So he's *my* boyfriend, not yours."

"True. But he's *my* friend and he wanted to know how I did on the test. I didn't even get to tell him since he wasn't in his room."

"Just a friend?" Mary Beth scoffed.

Lauren bristled. "That's right," she repeated. "In fact, he's the *only* friend who wanted to know how I did on my math test."

Mary Beth felt all the blood drain from her face. Her roommate did have a point. She'd totally forgotten. "Oh, Lauren," she said sincerely. "I'm sorry."

"No big deal." Lauren shrugged.

"You must think I'm a total jerk. That test was really important." She glanced hesitantly at her roommate. "So how did you do?"

"I got a D."

Ugh. Mary Beth had never gotten a D, but she knew they were definitely bad news at Foxhall.

"What are you going to do?"

Lauren shrugged again.

Mary Beth shifted uncomfortably. She felt like such a dork whining about Tommy when Lauren had real troubles. If Lauren failed math, she'd have to drop out of the afternoon riding program.

"Well, forget about math," Lauren said, trying to sound cheery. "That's not why I came over. Jina and I went to talk to Mrs. Caufield."

Mary Beth's mouth went dry. "You did?" she asked, hoping she sounded cool.

Lauren nodded. "We told her that you really wanted to be assigned the new horse."

Mary Beth suddenly felt confused. "But that's not what I heard you—" she blurted before stopping herself. She didn't want Lauren to know she'd been listening at the door.

"We both told her you can't wait to ride Fawn."

Can't wait to ride Fawn! Mary Beth's brows rose in sudden understanding. So that's what Lauren had been saying to Mrs. Caufield. She'd heard it all wrong!

Mary Beth dove for the door, swinging it wide. Grabbing her startled roommate, Mary Beth gave her a big hug.

"What's that for?" Lauren gasped.

"To say thank you for telling Mrs. Caufield how much I like Fawn!"

"You're welcome." Lauren pulled away, a puzzled smile on her face.

Mary Beth hopped around in a circle. "Do you and Jina really think I can handle Fawn?" she asked excitedly.

"Sure. And so does Andie." Lauren grinned. "Besides, we want you to become horse-crazy like us."

"Lauren!" Katherine Parks called from outside the open office door. "Mrs. Caufield wants to see you."

"I wonder what for?" Lauren turned back to Mary Beth. "See you back at the suite," she said and took off at a jog.

But Mary Beth barely heard her. She was too busy daydreaming.

A few minutes ago, she'd decided she didn't deserve Fawn. But now she knew that Lauren was right. She was ready. She wanted to be horse-crazy, too.

Later that afternoon, Mary Beth followed Andie into the suite. Her cheeks were chapped from the cold, and dust and Dan hairs covered her jacket.

With a tired sigh, she flopped down on her bed. Andie sat on the edge of her own bed and started to pull off her tall black boots.

"Who's got manure on their feet?" Jina asked from the bathroom doorway, wrinkling her nose. She was drying her face with a towel.

Mary Beth sniffed the air. "Must be Andie."

She pointed at her roommate.

"Mary Beth." Andie pointed at Mary Beth.

Jina laughed. "Gross. I bet you both do. You'd better clean it off. And where's Lauren? If she doesn't hurry, she'll be late for dinner."

Mary Beth sat up and bent over to unlace her jodhpur boots. "Lauren's talking to Mrs. Caufield."

"Again?" Jina went back into the bathroom, and Mary Beth heard running water.

"I heard you two guys told Mrs. Caufield I could handle Fawn," she called. "Thanks."

Andie snorted and a boot plopped on the floor. "*You* handle *Fawn*? That's a joke."

"No, it's not," Mary Beth said huffily. Standing up, she pulled off her coat, and horse hairs flew everywhere. "Katherine told Jina that Fawn's so well trained even a beginner could ride her."

"Yeah, but not a superklutz like you," Andie teased.

Just then the suite door opened and Lauren walked in, her helmet dangling from one hand. She looked really upset. Probably the math test, Mary Beth thought. She wished she could make her friend feel better.

"Isn't Fawn well trained?" Mary Beth asked

Lauren, hoping to take her mind off her problems. "Katherine said she's push-button."

Jina came out of the bathroom carrying her bath bucket. "She's dead quiet, too."

"Yeah. She's nice." Lauren said flatly. She slumped on her bed, her helmet hanging between her knees.

"So quiet even *I* can ride her," Mary Beth declared. "And she's so cute."

"Give me a break." Andie made a gagging noise.

Ignoring her, Mary Beth went over and sat down next to Lauren. "Tomorrow I'm going to ask Mrs. Caufield to assign Fawn to me. I'll tell her if she doesn't, I'll just *die*."

"Uh, I wouldn't do that if I were you, Mary Beth," Lauren said. Abruptly, she stood up and went over to the wardrobe. Flinging open the double doors, she studied the jumble of clothes inside.

"Why not?" Mary Beth asked, frowning.

"Yeah, why not?" Andie echoed. She'd stopped pulling off her boot to stare at Lauren. Even Jina was looking curiously at her.

"Because." Lauren turned to face them, the helmet still clutched in her fingers. "Because Mrs. Caufield assigned Fawn to *me*!"

7

"Mrs. Caufield assigned Fawn to *you*?" Mary Beth exclaimed in disbelief.

Lauren nodded.

Mary Beth opened her mouth, then shut it. She didn't know what to say.

Ever since she'd first seen Fawn, she'd dreamed about riding the new horse. And now her best friend was going to ride her instead.

Slowly, Mary Beth pulled off her jodhpur boots and let them drop to the floor. Jina and Andie were watching her with worried expressions as if they were afraid she was going to pick up a boot and whack Lauren with it.

But Mary Beth didn't know how to react.

"What about Whisper?" Jina asked Lauren. "You two were doing so great together."

"I know." Lauren's face crumpled. "I mean,

it's not like I asked to be assigned to Fawn."

"Hi, guys." Tiffany appeared in the doorway. Her hair was smoothed back by a blue hair band that matched the Foxhall blazer the girls had to wear to dinner. "Tommy's on the phone."

Mary Beth nodded mechanically. *Maybe talking to Tommy will help,* she thought. She felt like a robot as she stood up and started for the door.

"Uh, the call's not for you, Mary Beth," Tiffany said. "He wants to talk to Lauren."

Lauren! Totally taken aback, Mary Beth stopped dead in the middle of the room.

"Oh," Lauren said, her gaze darting nervously to Mary Beth. Then, with lowered eyes, she hurried past Tiffany and out the door.

For a second, no one said a word. Tiffany glanced from Jina to Andie to Mary Beth. "Is something wrong?" she asked.

Andie shrugged. "Maybe you better ask Mary Beth."

All eyes swung to Mary Beth. "No, nothing's wrong," she declared. "Nothing's wrong at all," she repeated, her voice cracking, "except that Lauren stole my horse *and* my boyfriend!"

"She didn't actually steal your horse," Jina

55

said. "There must be a reason Mrs. Caufield assigned Fawn to her instead of you."

Mary Beth didn't want to hear about any reasons. "I doubt it," she snapped at Jina. "I bet that when Lauren talked to Mrs. Caufield, she was mad because I yelled at her about calling Tommy, so she told Mrs. Caufield *she* wanted Fawn. Or maybe Dorothy told Mrs. Caufield how I almost rode Dan without reins and how his cooler fell off and he trampled it."

"You were going to ride without reins?" Andie smothered a snicker.

Mary Beth shot her a nasty look. "Well, even if Lauren didn't steal my horse, it sure looks like she stole my boyfriend!"

"You're right about that," Andie agreed.

"That Tommy guy on the phone is *your* boyfriend?" Tiffany asked, looking puzzled.

"He *was*," Mary Beth corrected. She jerked her Foxhall blazer from its hanger in the wardrobe. "Is anyone going to dinner?"

"Me!" Jina dashed over to get her blazer. Even Andie hurriedly put on her sneakers.

Mary Beth headed for the door just as Lauren came into the suite. Immediately, Mary Beth froze.

"So, did you have a nice chat with Tommy?"

she asked, her voice dripping with sarcasm.

"Yes, as a matter of fact I did," Lauren said. She stepped around Mary Beth without even looking at her.

"And did you tell him about the big fat D you got in math?" she asked loudly.

Lauren stiffened. "Yes."

"You got a *D*?" Andie exclaimed in disbelief.

Jina gasped. "Oh, Lauren. How could you get a D? Now you'll be kicked out of the riding program!"

"Gee, I don't think I've ever gotten such a bad grade," Tiffany said.

"Well, excuse me for being dumb," Lauren retorted, her blue eyes angry. "Not that any of you really care."

"Oh, I care." Mary Beth stuck her nose in Lauren's face. "Because if you flunk math, you'll get kicked out of riding. Then *I* can ride Fawn!"

As soon as the words were out, Mary Beth realized how horrible they sounded. But for some reason she didn't care. She wanted Lauren to feel as hurt as she did.

Lauren put her hands on her hips. "Thanks a bunch—all of you—for your sympathy. Especially since you were the ones who made me get that D."

"What do you mean?" Tiffany scrunched up her face.

"Yeah, how did we do that?" Andie demanded.

Lauren pointed at Andie. "All last week I made beds to earn money for *your* horse when I should have been studying." Her finger moved to Jina and Mary Beth. "The week before I busted my breeches so I could get a decent score on the knowledge test at the show because you guys were so hot to win. Then I've had to walk on eggshells because Mary Beth's been so jealous about Tommy. And last but not least"—she stabbed her finger at Tiffany—"all I heard this weekend was how we need an A on that stupid play!"

Pausing, Lauren took a deep breath, then rushed on. "And if that's not bad enough, the constant noise and bickering in this suite make it impossible to study. So *that's* why I flunked my stupid test!"

For a second, no one said a word.

Finally, Mary Beth broke the silence. "Well, if we're such terrible roommates, why don't you just move out?"

Lauren jerked her head as if she'd been slapped. Mary Beth caught her breath, suddenly realizing what she had said. But she knew it was too late to take the words back.

"Maybe I just will," Lauren said. There was a hurt expression in her eyes, but then they turned ice blue. Grabbing her blazer off the back of her desk chair, she started for the door. "I'll go ask Ms. Shiroo right now."

"Wait," Jina cried. Rushing over to Lauren, she put her hand on her roommate's arm. "Mary Beth didn't really mean that. She was just mad."

Lauren twisted to look at Mary Beth. Their eyes locked.

Tell her you didn't mean it, Mary Beth ordered herself. *Tell her you're sorry.*

But she couldn't. Maybe she did mean it. Maybe they really shouldn't be roommates anymore.

"No, I think Mary Beth's right," Lauren said, her voice flat. "If I'm going to raise my grades, it might be better for me to move out."

"You're really going to change suites?" Tiffany asked.

Lauren nodded, and Tiffany grinned. "Hey, why don't *I* move in here? You can move in

59

with my roommates. *All* they do is study."

"Great idea, Tiffany." Without looking at anyone, Lauren put on her blazer. Mary Beth had never seen her roommate's face so pale. "Let's go ask Ms. Shiroo. Right now."

"But—but—" Jina stammered. "You can't just move out. We've been roomies from the beginning. Right, Andie? Right, Mary Beth?"

Andie shrugged as she finished tying her shoe. "Maybe Lauren's right. Things have been pretty crazy in here lately. And we don't want her to flunk math."

Mary Beth didn't say anything. Her mind was a confused tangle.

Jina was right. They'd been roomies since the first day of school. Lauren had been her best friend. But now...

"So, it's settled then," Lauren said. "If Ms. Shiroo says it's okay, Tiffany and I will switch."

Before anyone could stop her, Lauren walked out the door.

"I can't believe you two didn't try and stop her!" Jina scolded Andie and Mary Beth. "Lauren's our friend. We can't let her *leave*."

Andie knotted her second shoelace and stood up. "It's not like she's gone forever. She'll still be living on the fourth floor. And maybe it'll be good for Lauren. Tiffany's roommates are real geeks. I bet she'll pull her grade up."

"Right," Mary Beth blurted. What Andie said made sense. "Then she can move back in with us."

Jina whirled on her, her golden eyes glittering. "Are you kidding? After what you said to her, Mary Beth, you'll be lucky if she ever speaks to you again."

All the blood rushed from Mary Beth's face. "Well, I—I was mad," she tried to explain.

Frowning, Jina put on her blazer. "No, you were mean."

Mary Beth swallowed hard. Jina usually wasn't so outspoken. But when she did speak up, she was usually right.

"Mary Beth wasn't *that* mean," Andie argued. "After all, Lauren did call Tommy behind her back."

Plunking down on the bed, Mary Beth put her face in her hands. "Lauren had a good reason for calling him," she mumbled, feeling worse by the minute.

"I thought so," Jina said. "And I bet there's a good explanation for why Mrs. Caufield assigned her Fawn, too."

"Well, Lauren did accuse all of us of making her flunk," Andie went on. "And she's probably right. We haven't made it easy for her to concentrate on studying."

Jina pursed her lips. "True. But we could have tried *helping* her out instead of *kicking* her out."

Andie and Mary Beth exchanged glances.

"Let's go find her," Mary Beth said, standing up. "We can tell her we don't want her to move. Maybe if I apologize a hundred times, she'll listen."

Andie stood up, too. "Okay, okay."

The three roommates headed down the hall to the suite where Ms. Shiroo, the dorm mother, lived. The hall was empty, since most of the girls had gone to dinner.

When they passed suite 4F, Mary Beth glanced in the room. Tiffany was coming out of the door, a pile of bedclothes in her arms.

"Hey, it's my new roommates coming to help!" she said happily.

Mary Beth stopped so fast that Jina plowed into her back. "What?"

Tiffany grinned over the heap of covers. "I'm starting to move some of my things into your room."

"You mean Shiroo gave you permission already?" Jina exclaimed.

Tiffany nodded excitedly. "She thought it was a great idea. She said you four probably needed splitting up anyway."

"What!" Andie screeched. "Why'd the old witch say that?"

"She said Lauren's guidance counselor had already talked to her about improving Lauren's 'study conditions.' "

"Where's Lauren?" Mary Beth peered over Tiffany's shoulder.

"She went to dinner with her sister."

Mary Beth felt as though someone had punched her in the stomach. They were too late!

"Hey, grab a pile of clothes." Tiffany nodded toward the stripped bed. The bare mattress was piled high with skirts, shirts, pants, and dresses.

Mary Beth stared at Tiffany in disbelief. "You're moving all that stuff into our suite?"

"Oh, not everything. Ms. Shiroo suggested we just switch rooms temporarily. Before we leave for Thanksgiving break, we're supposed to discuss whether we think the new arrangement's working out. Then I'll move *all* my things."

Andie snorted. "Well, I can tell you right now, if you've got more junk than that, it's not going to fit."

"Sure it will!" Tiffany said brightly, thrusting the bedclothes into Mary Beth's arms. "Here, you take this. Andie, Jina, come help me with this other stuff. I just know we're going to have oodles of fun together!"

Oodles? Mary Beth flashed Jina and Andie a pained look, but they followed Tiffany into the suite.

Mary Beth sighed. *This is all your fault, Finney*, she told herself as she struggled down the hall, the bedspread dragging on the floor.

"Can you believe how much junk Tiffany has?" Andie asked. She came up behind Mary Beth, carrying a makeup mirror.

"And I'll have to take my hair dryer, too," Tiffany was telling Jina, her voice echoing down the hall.

"That does it." Andie set the lamp down in the middle of the hall. "I'm not missing dinner so Tiffany can have gorgeous hairdos and enough matching outfits to last a month. Tiffany!" she called. "Move your own junk. I'm leaving!"

"Me too." Mary Beth hurried into their suite and threw the clothes on Lauren's bed.

"Wait for me," Jina called, darting from Tiffany's room.

"Hey, where are you guys going?" Tiffany called as she came out into the hall after Jina. "I only have a few more things!"

But Mary Beth, Jina, and Andie were already pounding down the stairs to the first floor of Bracken Hall. When they got outside, the three girls jogged across the courtyard. It was dark except for a few outdoor lights.

"Maybe if you throw yourself at Lauren's feet and beg forgiveness, she'll come back," Jina puffed as they sprinted down the sidewalk.

"No," Andie cut in. "Lauren has to *want* to come back. Otherwise it will never work."

Mary Beth wrapped her arms around her chest, trying to keep warm. "I'm really sorry, guys. This is all my fault."

"It sure is," Andie grumbled as they ran up the stairs to the front doors of Eaton Hall.

"It is not," Jina shot right back. "Lauren accused all of us of being lousy roommates, remember?"

Mary Beth opened the door. "What do you think we should do?"

"I don't know," Jina said. "But we have to think of *something*."

Mary Beth gave a gloomy sigh. "Yeah. We definitely have to do something. But what?"

She looked hopefully at Jina and Andie, but they only shrugged as they went into Eaton Hall. They didn't have any answers, either.

Later that night, Mary Beth lay in bed, her raggedy quilt pulled up to her chin. Wide awake, she stared at the ceiling. The room was dark but not silent. Tiffany snored like a pig.

And then there was that awful smell. Mary Beth wrinkled her nose. Before going to bed, Tiffany had sprayed the whole room with air freshener. Now it smelled like rotten fruit.

With a sigh, Mary Beth rolled onto her side. A shadowy blob glowered menacingly from the middle of the suite floor.

Mary Beth's heart raced. Then she remembered what it was—Tiffany's giant teddy bear.

Groaning, Mary Beth pulled her quilt over her head. Tiffany had insisted she couldn't be without the bear—and the hair dryer and the study pillow and the bed lamp and the poster of the Renegades...The list was endless.

Even worse, when they'd gotten back from dinner, they'd found that Lauren had already stripped her bed, taken her bath bucket and one change of clothes, and moved out.

Later, at eight o'clock sharp, the girls had practiced *Black Beauty's Hints* without Lauren. And it stunk as bad as the air freshener.

Mary Beth figured they'd all get a D on the English project. Then they'd all get kicked out of the riding program. Except Tiffany, of course.

A big wet tear rolled down Mary Beth's

cheek. As she wiped it away with the frayed edge her quilt, a megawave of homesickness washed over her. If only her mom and dad were there. They'd know what to do.

But her parents weren't there, and everything was messed up.

And it was all her fault.

9

"If I'd been you, Merrylegs," said Mary Beth, pretending to be Ginger in *Black Beauty's Hints*, "I would have given those boys a good kick." Lifting her leg, she kicked out behind her.

Twitters of amusement rose from the students in the sixth grade English class. It was Wednesday morning, and the girls were performing their play.

Next to Mary Beth, Andie clapped a hand over her mouth to keep from laughing, too. Mary Beth glowered at her. Okay, so their play was stupid, but Andie didn't have to make it worse.

"No doubt you would kick," said Tiffany, who played the pony Merrylegs. "But I am not such a fool as to anger the master. Uh—" she glanced down at the script that she held in front of her "—since I do love my sweetfeed."

The twitters grew louder.

"But you don't want Master to give you too much sweetfeed," Jina, who was Black Beauty, added. "And you don't want her to give it to you when you're hot, since you might get colic. Then Master would have to call the vet."

Andie couldn't keep her face straight. "And I, the vet, would give you medicine to make you do a giant horse poop," she muttered under her breath, but it was loud enough for the first row of girls to hear. They all cracked up.

"Did I miss something humorous?" Mrs. James asked from the back of the room.

Immediately, Jina piped up, "No, Mrs. James. Andie just forgot her lines."

"Andie!" Tiffany hissed. "Quit fooling around!"

"And I, the vet, would have to give you medicine," Andie said, her expression deadpan, "so Master Remick could ride you again." She turned to Lauren.

When Lauren didn't say anything, Mary Beth peered around Andie to see what was going on. Lauren was staring off into space.

"Master?" Mary Beth prompted.

Lauren turned toward her. "Hmm?"

"It's your line."

At that, Lauren flushed pink. "Oh, right. Uh, thank you, Black Beauty, for those helpful hints. Now I'll know how to take care of all my steeds so they'll be happy and healthy."

Mary Beth rolled her eyes with relief. Finally, it was over!

"Well," Mrs. James said as the girls shuffled back to their seats, "that was certainly interesting. I'm sure the class learned a lot about horses."

"And horse poop," Leanna, the girl in back of Mary Beth, snickered.

But Mary Beth didn't care. *One less thing to worry about,* she thought as her eyes focused on the back of Lauren's head. Now she could concentrate on figuring out how to apologize to Lauren. Even if her ex-roommate would never come back to suite 4B, Mary Beth still wanted to be her friend.

There was only one problem: Lauren would have to forgive her first.

"Half-seat position!" Mrs. Caufield instructed the four beginners lined up in the middle of the outside ring that afternoon.

Mary Beth groaned. Her ears were frozen, her fingers numb, and the half-seat position was a killer.

Leaning forward over the pommel, Mary Beth sunk her weight in her heels and tried to balance with her seat lifted slightly above the saddle. Instantly, she fell onto Dan's neck.

"Go ahead and grab the mane if you need to," Mrs. Caufield said as she walked up to Dan. Putting her hand on Mary Beth's right calf, she pushed her heel down even farther.

"Weight in your heels and thighs," she said. "And look straight ahead so your shoulders are lined up over your knees. There. Better?"

Mary Beth nodded grimly, then immediately tipped forward again. Mrs. Caufield gave her an encouraging pat on the leg. "It takes time."

Like forever, Mary Beth thought as Mrs. Caufield walked over to Heidi, who was perched perfectly on Windsor. Flopping back in the saddle, Mary Beth was going to give herself a rest. But then a flash of gold caught her eye. Lauren was riding Fawn down the drive to the indoor arena.

Mary Beth watched until they disappeared

into the arena. The two were made for each other, she realized. It was obvious why Mrs. Caufield had chosen Lauren to ride the new horse. Anyone could see that petite, graceful Lauren was perfect for Fawn.

Just like klutzy old Mary Beth Finney was perfect for Dan.

"Mary Beth," Jina said as she opened Dan's stall door half an hour later. "I found out why Mrs. Caufield assigned Fawn to Lauren."

"That's no big secret." Mary Beth lifted the saddle flap to unbuckle the girth.

Jina halted next to Dan's big head. "You know already?"

"Sure. Fawn and Lauren are perfect for each other." She let the girth hang, then, putting her hand under the pommel and cantle, slid the saddle and pad off Dan's broad back.

"No, that's not why." As Jina talked, she unbuckled the throatlatch on Dan's bridle. "You know Melanie Harden, the senior who's president of the Horse Masters Club?"

"I think so."

"She's looking for a horse to buy to take to college next year."

73

Mary Beth shifted the saddle in her arms. "Oh, yeah. Now I remember her." She wished Jina would hurry. The saddle was getting heavy. "Andie was really mad when Melanie rode Magic."

"Right, only he was too green. She wants a horse she can event."

"Event, huh?" Mary Beth said, even though she had no idea what Jina was talking about.

Jina slid the headpiece over Dan's head and the bit fell from his mouth. "So now Melanie's trying out Whisper."

"Whisper? Oh, I get it. If Melanie's riding Whisper, then Lauren doesn't have a horse for her lessons."

"Right." Jina put a halter on Dan.

"Yeah, but why did Mrs. Caufield have to assign her Fawn?"

Jina opened the stall door so the two of them could take the saddle and bridle to the tack room.

"There aren't any other horses," she explained. "Since that new girl Becky started riding, there aren't enough horses to go around."

"Oh," Mary Beth said when they reached the tack room. Compared to outside, the tack room was warm. After setting the saddle on its rack, she held her hands in front of the portable heater. "So that's why you haven't been riding this week."

Jina nodded. Her back was to Mary Beth as she hung up Dan's bridle. "Yeah. I've only been riding on Tuesdays and Thursdays when I go to Middlefield Stables."

"Boy, what a jerk I've been," Mary Beth murmured. She sighed and her shoulders slumped.

Jina joined her by the heater. For a minute, the two sat side by side on a tack trunk and warmed their hands.

"And the weird thing is, I'm not sure why I've been acting so crazy. Jealous and angry and mean." Mary Beth frowned down at her dirty fingers.

Jina shook her head. "I don't know what to tell you. You *have* been acting a little strange the last couple of weeks." She glanced sideways at Mary Beth. "Maybe you should talk to someone about it."

"Like who? At home, I could always talk to my mom and dad. But here..." Her voice trailed off.

"How about your counselor?"

"Mrs. Jacquin? I met with her about midterm grades."

"Well, the counselors are here for things besides grades. Look how Mr. Lyons helped Lauren deal with that whole Ashley mess earlier this year."

"True." Mary Beth stared off into space. Maybe talking to someone would help sort out her feelings. She sure needed to do something.

The tack room door banged open, and two older girls came in carrying saddles and bridles.

Mary Beth stood up. "I've got to go," she said to Jina, "before Dan thinks I abandoned him."

"So you think you'll talk to Mrs. Jacquin?" Jina asked as she walked out the door with Mary Beth.

Mary Beth nodded. For the first time in days, she felt a glimmer of hope. Things had to get better. They just had to.

10

"We've got to get Tiffany out of here," Andie said between clenched teeth. It was Wednesday night after dinner. Andie, Mary Beth, and Jina were lying around the suite, studying.

"What?" Mary Beth glanced up from the book *The Giver* she was reading for English class.

Dropping her notebook, Andie went over to Mary Beth's bed. Jina turned around in her desk chair.

"I said, we've got to get her out of here." Andie jerked her thumb toward the bathroom door. Behind it, Mary Beth heard loud, high-pitched singing.

"She *is* noisy," Jina admitted. "And what is that awful song she's singing?"

Andie looked shocked. "She's singing? I

thought someone was *murdering* her. Not that I'd be too upset."

Mary Beth giggled. "Oh, come on, Andie. She's not *that* bad."

"Not that bad!" Andie exclaimed. Jumping off the bed, she darted to the wardrobe and flung open the doors. "Look! Just look. She's hogged every inch!"

"Well, true," Mary Beth admitted. Tiffany's clothes took up two thirds of the wardrobe.

"And *this!*" Andie declared, waving toward Tiffany's bed. It was covered with a bright purple-flowered bedspread, a dozen matching pillows, and about ten stuffed animals. "She's only been here one day and her stuff is already creeping over to my side of the room. Pretty soon, her stupid, ugly bear will be sleeping in my bed."

Jina and Mary Beth started laughing.

Andie scowled. "It's not funny, guys."

"Well"—Jina exchanged glances with Mary Beth—"she does have a ton of stuff. And she sure can talk a lot. I think she showed me her photo album and her Young Miss Rescue Squad trophy a million times."

Mary Beth sighed. "It sure isn't the same

without Lauren. Do you think she likes Tiffany's roommates?"

"Who cares?" Andie scoffed. "I want her back in our suite."

"Me too." Jina eyed Andie. "So, why'd you change your mind? You were all for Lauren moving out."

"Well, that was before Tiffany moved in," Andie said darkly. "I bet her own roommates were thrilled to get rid of her."

Jina placed a finger on her lips. "Shhh. She'll hear you."

The singing had stopped.

"So what?" Andie retorted, but she lowered her voice. "We all want her to move out, right?"

"Right," Mary Beth whispered back. "But I learned my lesson with Lauren. We don't need to hurt her feelings."

"I agree," Jina said.

"Besides," Mary Beth continued, "tomorrow afternoon I have an appointment to see my counselor. Maybe she'll give me some ideas on how to get Lauren back—without making Tiffany feel bad."

"Oh, right." Andie frowned impatiently. "I'll give you until Thursday night to figure out what to do. But if Tiffany's not out by then, I'm throwing her and her stupid bear right out the window!"

"Come on in, Mary Beth." Mrs. Jacquin waved her into the office.

Eyes lowered, Mary Beth stepped into the large room. Since it was shared by three other math teachers, it was partitioned off into four cubicles.

Mrs. Jacquin's section had an antique oak desk and swivel chair. Several African violets grew in pots on a stand underneath the window that overlooked the garden behind Old House.

"What can I do for you?" Mrs. Jacquin gestured for Mary Beth to sit in a folding chair by the violets. Clutching her riding helmet, Mary Beth perched on the edge of the seat.

"Are you on your way to a lesson?" Mrs. Jacquin asked.

Mary Beth nodded. The math teacher was young and friendly, and Mary Beth knew she was trying to put her at ease. But Mary Beth couldn't relax. Before, she'd always had her parents to discuss her problems with. This was the first time she'd approached someone else.

Mrs. Jacquin smiled and sat down in the swivel chair. "Are you enjoying the lessons?"

Mary Beth fiddled with her helmet strap. "Yes. And no. I'm not very good at riding, so sometimes it gets frustrating."

Mrs. Jacquin nodded. "I can empathize with that. I've always been frightened of horses myself."

Mary Beth's chin snapped up and her hands stopped fiddling. "Really? I thought I was the only person at Foxhall who was scared of horses."

"Oh, no. Only about forty percent of our students are enrolled in the riding program. That means at least sixty percent either don't like to ride, or"—she bent closer—"they might even be scared."

Mary Beth grinned. She'd never thought of it that way before.

Rotating in her chair, Mrs. Jacquin opened a folder on her desk. "Is there something in particular you wanted to discuss? I checked your grades and progress reports, and I didn't see anything awry with your academic performance."

"It's not my grades," Mary Beth said. She hesitated, and her gaze shot down to her hands again.

"Let me guess. Roommate problems?"

Slowly, Mary Beth nodded.

"And I bet you're homesick, too. I remember meeting your mom and dad during Parents' Weekend. You seemed very close. It must be hard for you to be away for so long."

Mary Beth nodded again. Then, suddenly, tears started rolling down her cheeks. Dropping her helmet, Mary Beth put her palms over her face and sobbed. Harder and harder she cried, until her shoulders shook with the flood of tears that spilled onto her jeans like raindrops.

Mrs. Jacquin came over and placed a comforting hand on Mary Beth's arm. Still, she couldn't stop, even when her nose ran and her eyes stung with the salty tears.

Finally, the sobs turned into hiccups. Mrs. Jacquin handed her a fistful of tissues. Mary Beth wiped her face, then blew her nose. With a shuddering breath, she peered up at the counselor.

"Sorry," she whispered.

Mrs. Jacquin smiled gently. "There's nothing to be sorry about. You needed to cry. And you also need to realize that you aren't the only student at Foxhall who misses her family."

"I guess I didn't realize how much I missed them." She dabbed at her eyes. "I mean, my roommates don't seem to get homesick."

"Each student is different. Some girls have been in boarding schools before. Or they've been away for a whole summer at camp."

"And some don't have much of a home life, I guess," Mary Beth murmured, thinking about Andie and Jina.

"That's right. Often, if there are big problems at home, Foxhall is a safe haven for those girls."

"But my parents have always been there for me," Mary Beth said. "I even miss my bratty brothers and sister."

Mrs. Jacquin gave her another pat. "That's why the separation is even harder. And sometimes that's why roommate problems crop up."

Mary Beth looked up at her, puzzled.

"I've been a counselor now for six years at Foxhall, so I've mediated all kinds of roommate troubles." Mrs. Jacquin made a steeple with her fingers. "Tell me about yours."

"Well..." Taking another deep breath, Mary

Beth told Mrs. Jacquin the whole story. "Jina thought I should talk to you, since I'm so confused. It's just not like me to push away a friend over a horse or a guy."

"Did you have close friends at home?" Mrs. Jacquin asked.

Mary Beth thought about Janie, her best friend at home. "Yes."

"And what happened when you two got into fights?"

"I'd tell my mom about it."

"Did you have a boyfriend?"

Brad? Mary Beth scrunched up her face. "Sort of."

"And when you felt jealous or sad because of something a boy you liked said or you had problems at school, what did you do?"

"Sometimes I'd talk about it with my parents or even blow up at them. Or sometimes, if I was in a really crummy mood, I'd kick my sister out of my room or I'd hold down my brother until he said uncle." She grinned sheepishly. "But we always made up. I mean, we love each other and everything."

Mrs. Jacquin nodded knowingly. "That's what families are for. Especially parents—to

84

love you no matter what. But here at school, when you're upset or mad, you don't have a mom or dad or brother, so you—"

"Take things out on my roommates?" Mary Beth guessed.

"I think so. Lauren was your best friend and the person you were closest to. But, remember, Lauren has her own troubles, so she couldn't handle your blowups. Your mom would have listened to your outburst, then given you a hug and said it was okay. Lauren just felt hurt."

Mary Beth bit her lip. "Do you think there's a chance we can make up?"

"I hope so. But from now on, Mary Beth, when things get you down, come to me, okay?" Mrs. Jacquin smiled. "I promise I'll listen no matter how angry you are. In fact"—she leaned back in her chair—"Mrs. Thaney and I have been talking about starting a support group for sixth-graders next semester. Would you join?"

"I guess so..." Mary Beth said reluctantly. It would be hard talking about personal things in front of a bunch of other girls. Still, if it would help her keep her friends...

"Yes," she corrected. "I would come."

"Good. Would you like me to talk to Lauren for you?"

Mary Beth shook her head. "No. I think I need to do that myself. I just have to figure out a way to get her to listen!"

I'm going to fall, I just know it, Mary Beth thought as she gripped Dan's mane and trotted toward the pole on the ground. *Dan will jump and I'll land on the ground with a big splat.*

"Maintain your half-seat position!" Mrs. Caufield hollered to the line of beginners headed up the middle of the arena toward the pretend jump. "And when your horse trots over the pole, keep your hands firmly on its neck."

Mary Beth was at the end of the line, following Heidi on Windsor. *Heels down, sit up, weight in your thighs,* she recited, trying to convince herself she'd be fine. But when Dan was ten feet from the standards, she panicked and squeezed her eyes shut.

She could feel Dan rise and fall slightly. Then she heard a *clomp-clomp* sound, and the big horse slowed to a walk. Mary Beth opened her eyes again. Heidi, Shandra, and Becky were all watching her.

"Good, Mary Beth," Mrs. Caufield said, chuckling a bit. "But keep your eyes open next time."

At that, everybody burst out laughing. Even Mary Beth had to smile. It *was* funny. And after talking to Mrs. Jacquin, she'd decided she needed to lighten up.

"Let's try it again," Mrs. Caufield told the group. "After you go over the pole in the half-seat position, circle and trot over the pole again while posting. Any questions?"

Mary Beth raised her hand. "Is it all right if I lead?"

Mrs. Caufield arched one brow. "Why, sure."

"I bet lazy old Dan thinks it's a lousy idea," Heidi said in a low voice.

Ignoring her, Mary Beth urged Dan into a walk, kicking him once with her heels to remind him that she was the boss. When he trotted toward the standards, she looked straight ahead. And when Dan picked up his feet to step over the pole, Mary Beth felt a tingle of excitement.

"Very nice!" Mrs. Caufield called. "Circle and do it one more time. Then you're through for the day."

Mary Beth grinned as she posted briskly down the side of the arena. *Up down, up down.* It felt so natural now. She remembered the first time she'd trotted Dan. She'd bounced sky high.

I've really improved, Mary Beth told herself. *And even better, I'm having fun!*

"Gee, Mary Beth," Shandra said after the lesson, "I'm impressed." Side by side, the two girls were walking toward the barn, leading their horses. Shandra had been riding Teddy Bear, a fuzzy large pony. "I wish I had your determination."

"What do you mean?"

"Well, you just dig right in and do your best, no matter what. I admire that a lot."

Halting Dan, Mary Beth looked at Shandra in surprise. "Really?"

"Sure," Shandra said. "You've worked the hardest in our group. And I think you're going to be the best rider."

Pleased, Mary Beth bit back a grin. "You're doing great, too."

Shandra shrugged. "Oh, I don't know. I was thinking about dropping riding and taking up dance next semester."

"Why?"

"Well, riding's a lot of work." Shandra wrinkled her nose as they started up the hill again. "And it's dirty and cold. I always have manure on my shoes and horsehair on my clothes."

"True." Mary Beth thought back to the beginning of the week. Hadn't she been thinking the exact same things? But now she felt different. *Riding* felt different. *Maybe I'm not totally horse crazy yet*, Mary Beth thought to herself, *but I'm getting there.*

"Lauren?" Mary Beth poked her nose into Fawn's stall. The palomino mare had been eating her hay, but when she saw Mary Beth, she came over and snuffled her fingers.

Mary Beth stroked her velvety nose, then scratched behind her ears. "You really are cute. And maybe someday I'll even get to ride you. When I can canter better," she added quickly, "so I don't bounce on your back and pop you in the mouth."

Fawn nudged Mary Beth's arm with her nose, then went back to eating hay. Since the mare had been fed and was wearing her blanket, Mary Beth figured Lauren was finished for the afternoon. She must have just missed her.

Mary Beth sighed in exasperation. She'd figured out exactly what she was going to say, too.

"Ready for chow?" Andie called. She was coming out of the tack room, carrying her riding helmet.

"I'm starved." Mary Beth fell into step beside her roommate. "But I really want to talk to Lauren before dinner."

"Oh?" Andie glanced sideways at her as they headed down the drive toward the main buildings. "And ruin both your appetites? We're having baked ham and cherry pie."

Mary Beth's mouth started to water. "Sounds good. But tonight's the last night before Lauren has to make up her mind about staying in her new suite. I want to persuade her to move back."

"Want me to go with you?"

Mary Beth shook her head. "Thanks, but let me talk to her first. It was mostly my fault she moved out in the first place."

"Okay," Andie agreed. "If Lauren tells you she hates your guts and you're too upset to eat, can I have your pie?"

Mary Beth chuckled. "Sure."

When they reached the dorm, Mary Beth decided to take a shower before dinner. *You're stalling,* she told herself as the spray beat on her face.

She finished rinsing her hair and, after turning off the water, stepped from the shower.

"Are you in there, Mary Beth?" Tiffany called through the closed door.

"Yes."

"Good!" The door flew open and Tiffany burst in. Grabbing a towel, Mary Beth quickly wrapped it around herself.

Totally ignoring Mary Beth's embarrassment, Tiffany waved a notebook under her nose. "Guess what?" she sang out.

"Tiffany!" Mary Beth fumed. "Do you always barge into the bathroom on people?"

"Just when I've got great news," Tiffany replied cheerfully. She flipped back her hair with one hand.

I hate it when she does that, Mary Beth

thought. "It'd better be great news," she said through clenched teeth.

"We got a B."

"A *B!*" Mary Beth's jaw dropped in surprise. "On our English project?"

Tiffany nodded excitedly. "Yes. Mrs. James said it was the most original play she'd ever read."

"Let me see that." Mary Beth snatched the script from Tiffany's fingers and opened it to the back page. A for originality. C for presentation. B overall. "I can't believe it," Mary Beth murmured. "How'd you get this?"

"I stopped by Mrs. James's office after school. I'm dying to tell the others."

Mary Beth looked up sharply. "Can I tell Lauren?"

Tiffany frowned. "Why?" she asked.

Mary Beth hesitated. Did Tiffany have any idea they wanted her to move out?

"I need a peace offering," Mary Beth said, which was true. "Lauren may not be my roommate anymore, but I'd still like her to be my friend."

Tiffany pursed her lips and flipped her hair back again. "Oh, all right. But let me tell Andie and Jina."

"Sure," Mary Beth agreed, handing her back the play. "Jina isn't back from Middlefield Stables yet," she added, but Tiffany had already dashed from the room.

Mary Beth dressed quickly. The English grade would give her a good excuse to see Lauren. And once they were face to face, Lauren would just have to listen.

Fifteen minutes later, Mary Beth marched down the hall to suite 4F. The door was closed. Had Lauren and her roommates gone to dinner already?

She checked her watch. It was still early. She raise her fist and knocked.

The door flew open. Jeanine Watkins, a stocky eighth-grader, glared out at her. She was at least a foot taller and two feet wider than Mary Beth.

"What do you want?" Jeanine said, making the sentence sound like one word.

"Is Lauren here?"

"Yeah." Jeanine crossed her arms, taking up the whole doorway.

Mary Beth tried to see around the large girl, but every time she moved, Jeanine moved with her.

"Can I talk to her?"

"No."

"Oh." Mary Beth cleared her throat, and awkwardly shifted from foot to foot. "But I have something really important to tell her."

Jeanine bent closer. "And I have something important to tell you: *Get lost.* Lauren said she doesn't want to see anyone from suite 4B."

Before Mary Beth could protest, Jeanine slammed the door in her face.

"Hey!" Mary Beth banged on the door. "Open up! I have to talk to Lauren. It's an emergency."

Stepping back, she waited. The door to suite 4F didn't open.

"What's the matter, Finney?" someone hollered from the room across the hall.

"None of your business." Furious, Mary Beth kicked the doorjamb. "Ow!" Grabbing her toe, she hopped around on one foot. She'd forgotten she wasn't wearing shoes.

When she hobbled into suite 4B, Tiffany and Andie didn't even look up. They were sitting side by side on Andie's bed, studying the play.

"If you hadn't been such a big mouth, we probably would have gotten a B on presentation," Tiffany was complaining to Andie.

"Well, it wouldn't have changed our overall grade anyway," Andie pointed out.

"Excuse me," Mary Beth cut in. "I'm sorry I'm interrupting this totally important conversation, but, Tiffany, *what* is *wrong* with your old roommates?"

Tiffany finally glanced up. "Huh?"

Mary Beth limped over to stand in front of them. "What's with your old roommates? Especially that Jeanine girl."

"Oh, Jeanine's really sweet."

Mary Beth made a face. "Sweet? Are we talking about the same person?"

"I take it your little chat with Lauren didn't turn out so well." Andie chuckled. "What happened? Did sweetie-pie Jeanine throw you out of the room?"

"No. She just slammed the door in my face. But that's not going to stop me from apologizing to Lauren. I'm going right back down there and kick the door in—as soon as I put on shoes."

"Mary Beth Finney! Telephone!" someone called down the hall.

"Great." Turning, Mary Beth hobbled to the phone. She hoped it was her mother so she could complain about her obviously broken toe.

"Hello?"

"Well, it's about time I got to talk to you."

Mary Beth frowned. "Who's this?" She didn't recognize the voice at all.

"It's me, Janie. Remember me? Your best friend from Cedarville?"

"Janie!" Mary Beth said happily. "This is so cool! I was just telling my counselor about you today."

"That's nice. We all figured you'd forgotten your old friends in Cedarville."

"Never," Mary Beth declared.

"Then how come you never called Brad back?"

"Brad?" Mary Beth frowned. "He called? When?"

"Once yesterday, then again today."

Mary Beth's heart began to pound. She hadn't heard from Brad in ages. She wasn't sure he even liked her anymore.

"Wow. What did he want?"

"He wanted to ask you to go to the fall mixer at school this Saturday. He knew you'd be home for Thanksgiving vacation."

Mary Beth grabbed the phone cord excitedly. "He wants to ask me to the dance?"

"He *did*. But you never called back, so he asked Emily Zentz instead."

"Oh, no," Mary Beth said. She couldn't believe it. How could this have happened? "Did he leave a message?"

"Both times."

"Who'd he talk to?"

"Some girl named Lauren who said she'd give you the message right away."

Lauren! Mary Beth almost dropped the receiver.

"Are you there, Mary Beth?"

"I'm here," Mary Beth replied, trying to stay calm. "And I really didn't get the messages. Tell Brad I'm sorry for not calling him back."

They talked for a few more minutes, then hung up. For a moment, Mary Beth stood stiffly by the phone, unaware of the chattering girls leaving for dinner.

Then she abruptly spun on her stockinged feet and headed back down the hall to suite 4F.

"Oh, Lauren!" she called through the door with fake sweetness. "That little rat," she muttered to herself.

She listened. There was no reply, but she

knew the girls were in there. She hadn't seen any of them leave for dinner.

Mary Beth leaned closer to the door. "I know you're there, Lauren. So listen up. I want to thank you for not giving me my phone messages. Not only did you steal my boyfriend Tommy, but you ruined my chances with Brad, too. So if you were expecting me to apologize—forget it." Her voice rose to an angry shout. "Because as far as I'm concerned, you can stay in suite 4F forever!"

I'm such a jerk, Mary Beth thought glumly as she picked listlessly at her cherry pie. *Now Lauren will never forgive me.*

It was dinnertime. Mary Beth was seated at a round table set with linen napkins, crystal goblets, and real silverware, but she still didn't feel like eating.

"Hey, if you don't want your pie, pass it over here," Andie said. She was sitting next to Mary Beth, which was unusual. Since dinners were formal the girls had assigned seats that were changed every week. The idea was to get students from different dorms and grades to mingle.

Without a word, Mary Beth pushed the

plate over to Andie. "Help yourself."

"I will." Andie speared the pie with her fork and stuffed a huge bite in her mouth. "Mmmmm. You don't know what you're missing." She licked a glob of cherry off her lips.

"Yes, I do." Mary Beth sighed. "I love cherry pie. I'm just too upset to eat. How could I have yelled at Lauren like that?"

"You were mad."

Mary Beth snorted. "That's for sure. I can't believe Lauren didn't give me my messages from Brad."

"Are you sure Lauren was the one who answered the phone?"

"That's what Janie said Brad said."

Andie forked up another bite. "Well, if you ask me, Janie's wrong. Even if Lauren was furious at you, she never would have done something as low as that."

Mary Beth frowned. "But why would Janie lie?"

Andie shrugged. "Maybe she didn't. Maybe she or Brad heard the name wrong. Anyway, you could have at least let Lauren explain before chewing her out."

"Yeah, I know," Mary Beth said glumly, resting her chin in her hands.

"Manners, Mary Beth," Mr. Lyons, the gym teacher, reminded her from the other side of the floral centerpiece. Quickly Mary Beth whipped her elbows off the table.

Leaning back slightly in her chair, Mary Beth scanned the room for Lauren. Three rows away, she spotted her long blond braid. She could hear shrill laughter coming from the table.

She's probably telling everybody how I tried to kick the door down, Mary Beth thought.

"What are you going to do now?" Andie slid back Mary Beth's empty plate. It had been scraped clean.

Mary Beth sighed again. "I'll try to talk to her again after dinner."

"Ummm. An original plan," Andie teased.

"You have a better one?"

"Yeah. Send her a dozen red roses and a box of chocolates. It works in all those old movies."

Mary Beth eyed the centerpiece. The flowers were definitely fake. Still...

Mr. Frawley, Foxhall's headmaster, stood up to give his after-dinner speech. Tonight, it was about rejoining families for Thanksgiving. Mary Beth listened with only one ear. She was too busy plotting how to grab a silk rose. When the speech was over, Mr. Frawley began to dismiss the tables one by one. Mary Beth jiggled her foot impatiently, her eyes darting around the room. No one was looking. Furtively, she leaned across the table, moving her hand closer and closer to the vase.

"Table six may now leave."

Mary Beth snapped her hand back and stood up. *Too late.*

Mary Beth crossed the dark courtyard with Andie. "I sure wish I could have gotten one of those fake flowers for Lauren," Mary Beth said.

Stopping in the shadows, Andie reached inside her blazer and pulled out a red rose.

"How'd you get that?" Mary Beth gasped.

Andie grinned. "Easy. Now hurry up and get over to Lauren's suite before study hours start. Her table was dismissed first."

"Thanks, Andie." Mary Beth flashed her a grateful smile before taking off for Bracken Hall. As she leaped up the stairs, she thought about what she wanted to say to Lauren.

Just tell her the truth. Tell her you're sorry.

The door to suite 4F was wide open. Mary

Beth peeked cautiously inside. Jeanine and two of her other roommates were settling down to study. Lauren was nowhere in sight.

"Where's Lauren?" Mary Beth asked.

Jeanine gave her a sullen look, but one of the other girls answered, "We don't know. She left the dining hall with her sister."

Lauren's older sister, Stephanie, lived in Bracken Hall, too. Mary Beth rushed downstairs to the third floor. But when she reached Stephanie's room, Lauren had already gone.

"She left to study with her tutor. She has permission to spend extra time out of the dorm tonight," Stephanie said. Lauren's sister was tall, blond, and model-gorgeous.

"What's going on with you two, anyway?" Stephanie went on. "After dinner, Lauren couldn't stop crying. I've never seen her so upset. She's mad at you guys, and she *hates* her new roommates."

"It's a long story," Mary Beth said. But as she turned to leave, she had a glimmer of hope. If Lauren hated her new roommates, then maybe she could be convinced to come back.

Clattering down the steps, Mary Beth ran into the common room. She breathed a sigh of relief when she saw Ms. Shiroo.

"Yes, Mary Beth, you may go find Lauren," the dorm mother said. "I know how important this roommate issue is to you girls. But come right back and get to your own homework."

"Thanks!" Mary Beth sprinted from the room and out the exit door. She was pretty sure Lauren's tutor roomed in Mill Hall. Mary Beth couldn't remember the girl's name, but she knew she and Lauren studied in the common room.

She ran all the way to Mill Hall. When she burst into the common room, a tall, dark-haired girl looked up from where she was sitting on the sofa, reading. Mary Beth recognized her as Lauren's tutor and suddenly remembered her name.

"Hi, JoAnn. Where's Lauren?"

JoAnn shrugged. "I don't know. She hasn't shown up yet." The girl checked her watch. "And she's fifteen minutes late, too."

"Late? But where can she be? I checked her room."

Mary Beth stood frozen in the middle of the room. Panic began to crawl up her insides.

She thought back to her conversation with Stephanie. Lauren had left her sister still feeling really upset. Had she gone to some secret place where she could cry alone even though she knew it meant breaking Foxhall rules?

No. Mary Beth told herself. Lauren was too levelheaded. Or was she? Had all the craziness lately pushed her into doing something dumb?

If so, then it was all Mary Beth's fault.

Turning, Mary Beth raced from Mill Hall. She had to find Lauren!

13

"Lauren's gone!" Mary Beth blurted as she burst into suite 4B.

"What?" Andie dropped the book she'd been reading and sat bolt upright on her bed. "What do you mean, she's *gone*?"

Tiffany and Jina were both sitting at their desks, studying. Jina swung around with a worried look.

"She's not with her sister or in her room or studying with her tutor."

"You don't think she did something stupid, like run away?" Jina asked slowly.

"I don't know. But Stephanie said she was really upset." Dashing to the wardrobe, Mary Beth flung open the doors and started throwing clothes onto the floor.

"What are you doing?" Tiffany squeaked.

"You're making a mess."

"I'm trying to find my jeans." Mary Beth replied in a muffled voice. "I'm going to look for her. It's all my fault she disappeared. I'm the jerk that accused her of not giving me those stupid phone messages from Brad."

Suddenly, Tiffany covered her face with her hands and burst into tears.

Startled, Mary Beth, Jina, and Andie turned to stare at her.

"Hey, everything will be okay, Tiffany," Jina said in a soothing voice. "We'll find Lauren."

Tiffany only sobbed louder. "No, it won't. It's *my* fault that Lauren ran away."

"What?" The three roommates chorused. They all exchanged puzzled glances.

Climbing off the bed, Andie handed Tiffany a tissue. "Would you quit all that boo-hooing and tell us what you're talking about?"

Tiffany nodded, then blew her nose so hard it honked. When she finally stopped crying, she looked up at Mary Beth with bloodshot eyes. "I'm the one who didn't give you those phone messages." Her voice was so low that Mary Beth almost couldn't hear her.

"You! But why? Why did you tell Brad you were Lauren?"

"Because"—Tiffany sniffled—"yesterday I heard you guys saying that you didn't want me to be your roommate. So when Brad called, I decided to pretend I was Lauren. I knew it would make you mad at her. I hoped it would make you mad enough not to want her back..." Her voice trailed off as she stared down at the tissue crumpled in her hands.

Jina groaned. "What a mess!"

"I don't have time to deal with this now. I'm going to find Lauren." Mary Beth whirled into action. Grabbing her jeans from the bottom of the wardrobe, she tugged them on under her skirt.

She heard the scrape of a chair and in an instant Jina was beside her. "No way. Not without telling Ms. Shiroo. This is serious, Mary Beth. If Lauren did run away, we need help finding her."

"But if she didn't run away, and she's just hiding somewhere, we'll get her in big trouble if we rat on her," Mary Beth insisted.

"Look," Andie cut in, "I have to agree with Jina on this one. If we explain everything to Shiroo, I think we can count on her to help us without getting Lauren in trouble."

"Okay," Mary Beth agreed finally. She took

109

off her blazer and skirt and pulled on the old coat she used for riding. "You guys go down and tell Ms. Shiroo. But I'm heading outside to look for Lauren."

"Would this help?" Tiffany held up a flashlight she'd pulled out of her desk drawer. She looked so miserable, it made Mary Beth feel bad.

"Yeah. That will help a lot." She gave Tiffany a quick smile. "And don't blame yourself, okay? It's my fault this happened."

A few minutes later, Mary Beth was hurrying down the sidewalk toward Old House. Her hands were stuffed in her coat pockets, her fingers crossed. She hoped she would find Lauren in one of the offices talking to a counselor or in the infirmary with Mrs. Zelinski, the nurse.

But the main doors of the administration building were locked tight. Switching on the flashlight, Mary Beth jogged around to the side. Those doors were locked, too.

Mary Beth glanced around the dark parking lot. Where would Lauren go if she was upset?

Slowly, she walked toward the wooden and stone arch that connected the library with Old

House. A cold wind howled across the courtyard. Mary Beth shivered, remembering the stories all the new students were told about Sarah Pendleton, the Foxhall Academy ghost.

Any other time, she'd be too scared to go wandering around the campus alone. But tonight she was too worried to be frightened.

The wind caught a piece of notebook paper and blew it against Mary Beth's leg. Stooping, she picked it up. She was about to crumple it up and put it in her pocket when she noticed Lauren's name written at the top.

It was one of her math papers!

Mary Beth's heart pounded. She checked the date on the paper. November sixteenth. That meant Lauren had dropped the paper today.

But when? The paper was clean, so it couldn't have been lying on the ground for long. Had Lauren come this way? And why? Where had she gone?

Mary Beth glanced around, her gaze stopping at the hill leading up the stables. *The barn!*

Of course. Sometimes Mrs. Caufield or Katherine or Dorothy worked late. And Lauren knew the riding instructors well enough to talk over her problems with them. Maybe she'd even gotten permission to be at the barn after hours.

Mary Beth started up the hill at a jog. When she reached the top, she stopped to catch her breath. Frowning, she studied the barn area. It looked totally deserted. The only light came from the mercury-vapor lamp that shone over the driveway.

Mary Beth hesitated. It sure didn't look as if anyone was in the barn. Still, she wanted to check before heading back to the dorm.

"Lauren?" she called softly as she came down the barn aisle, swinging her flashlight from side to side. Stopping in front of Mrs. Caufield's office, she knocked, then tried the door. It was locked.

Then she heard a creak, and tingles of fear raced up her arms. *Go back,* she told herself as her heart beat wildly. *Lauren's not here.*

Just as Mary Beth turned around, the wind whipped around the corner of the barn and she heard the creak again. It sounded like a door that wasn't latched.

She aimed her flashlight down the aisle. As far as she could see, the top doors of the stalls were secured. What had been left open?

She took a step past the office. *Creak-k-k.*

The eerie sound sent shivers up her spine. Then something moved. Mary Beth gasped and jerked the light to her right. It was the tack room door. Someone had left it open.

Mary Beth exhaled in relief. Quickly, she ran to close it. Then it hit her—Dorothy always double-checked everything before leaving for the night. Had the wind forced it open?

A *bump* came from inside the tack room. Mary Beth recoiled from the open door. *You've got to get out of here*, she told herself again.

Slowly, she reached for the knob. But before she could shut the door, she heard the bumping noise again. Her hand froze. Her heart practically stopped beating.

Something was in the tack room!

Mary Beth couldn't move. She was too scared to run.

She swallowed hard, then blinked. A faint beam from the flashlight spilled into the tack room. Mary Beth willed herself to take just one glance before she slammed the door shut and raced for the safety of the dorm.

Nothing's in there, she told herself as her gaze skimmed the room. *Nothing,* she repeated as her numb brain suddenly realized what was wrong. There really was *nothing* in the tack room!

Mary Beth was so surprised, she forgot to be afraid. Stepping into the tack room, she flicked on the light. As she looked around, her mouth fell open.

The rows of saddle racks and bridle brackets were empty. Every piece of tack was gone!

14

Mary Beth stood in shocked silence, trying to make sense of the empty room. Had someone stolen the tack? If so, what had they done with twenty saddles and bridles?

A loud thump startled her. Mary Beth forced herself to look at the rectangular tack trunk in the far corner. The thump had come from there.

Sweat broke out on her forehead as she heard a moan rise from the closed box.

Someone was in the trunk!

Leave now! Mary Beth's mind screamed as visions of trapped ghosts filled her head. Then she realized how stupid that idea was.

"Mrs. Caufield?" Mary Beth croaked. "Are you in there?"

The moans turned into frantic grunts.

Dropping her flashlight, Mary Beth rushed over. She unlatched the top of the trunk and threw it open. Frightened blue eyes stared back at her.

"*Lauren!*" Mary Beth gasped. Reaching in, she tried to help her friend out. But Lauren's wrists and ankles had been bound with lead ropes. Her mouth had been covered with shipping bandages.

"Oh, Lauren, what happened?" Mary Beth tugged at the tight knots.

"Mmmph." Lauren shook her head from side to side, trying to communicate.

"Oh, right." Bending over the lip of the trunk, Mary Beth unpinned the bandages and unwrapped them from Lauren's head.

When she was free, Lauren exhaled loudly. Her skin was red and blotchy. "They stole all the tack!" she gasped, trying to struggle to a sitting position.

"Who?" Mary Beth pulled her upright, then started on the wrist ropes.

"Pete Previtti."

Mary Beth glanced sharply at Lauren. "The guy who hauls horses for Foxhall?"

"Yes. He thought I didn't see him, but I did. The creep. He was with one other guy I didn't recognize. A big ugly guy with bad skin." She shuddered. "He was the one who tied me up and dumped me in here."

"What were you doing at the barn?" Mary Beth tugged hard at the knot. Finally, it loosened, and she unwound the rope from Lauren's wrists.

Lauren rubbed her skin briskly. "Oooo, that feels better. I was upset, so I came to talk to Mrs. Caufield. I saw lights and figured she was still here. Only it was truck headlights instead. They'd aimed them into the tack room so they could see to move the stuff."

Bending, Lauren helped Mary Beth work on her ankle ropes. "And stupid me walked right up and asked those guys what they were doing. They were almost as surprised as I was. Anyway," she added grimly, "before I could run, they grabbed me."

"We've got to get help," Mary Beth said, undoing the last knot. Putting a hand under Lauren's arm, she helped her up.

Lauren winced in pain. "It feels like I've been in there forever. It's lucky you came up here and found me." She glanced curiously at Mary Beth. "What are *you* doing here?"

Mary Beth helped Lauren out of the trunk.

"I'll tell you everything on the way down to the dorm."

Mary Beth finished her story as she and Lauren hurried up the steps to Bracken Hall. She'd told Lauren everything.

"So when you disappeared, I figured you might have run away."

Lauren shook her head. "I never even heard you yelling through my door. I must have gone to dinner already."

"You're kidding!" Mary Beth blushed furiously.

"It's just as well you thought I did hear," Lauren said quickly. "Otherwise you wouldn't have come looking for me. I might have been stuck in that tack trunk forever!"

Mary Beth paused at the door. "You're right. It did turn out okay."

Feeling shy, she glanced down at her feet. "I want to say one more thing, though." Tears filled her eyes and she choked back a sob. "You're my best friend, Lauren. I never meant to hurt you. I'm really sorry I acted like such a jerk."

"Me too." Lauren gave her an awkward hug. "I mean, I'm sorry *I've* been a jerk."

"But you weren't. You were just worried about math." Mary Beth gave a big sigh of relief. "Let's promise *never* to get angry at each other again. Okay?"

Lauren nodded. "Okay. Uh, do you think Tiffany will be too upset when I tell her I want to switch back to suite 4B?"

Mary Beth grinned. "You really want to move back?"

Lauren nodded.

"Great! That goes for me and Andie and Jina, too. We all missed you." Mary Beth couldn't stop smiling. "And Tiffany knew the switch might only be temporary, right?"

"Right. Actually, I think her roommates would like her back." Lauren giggled. "They're all so boring—I think Tiffany livened the place up."

Just then the double doors burst open, nearly knocking Mary Beth off the steps.

"Where have you guys been?" Andie demanded.

Jina was right behind her, a frantic expression on her face. "We were about to call the police!"

"Well, we definitely *should* call them," Mary Beth said. "But first we have to talk to Ms.

Shiroo right away."

"Why? What happened?" Jina's eyes darted from Lauren to Mary Beth.

"Oh, nothing much," Mary Beth said. Wearily, she trudged past Andie and Jina and into the dorm. "Lauren was just tied up and locked in a trunk while Pete Previtti stole all the tack."

"Sure," Andie scoffed as she followed Mary Beth and Lauren. "Now tell us what *really* happened."

Friday morning, Mary Beth found a note on the memo board which hung outside their door.

TO: ANDIE, JINA, MARY BETH, AND LAUREN. PLEASE SEE MRS. CAUFIELD AFTER BREAKFAST.

"Do you think she found out what happened to the tack?" Jina asked from behind Mary Beth.

"Let's hope so." Mary Beth hurried back into the room. When she saw Lauren making her own bed as usual, happiness washed over her.

It had taken more than an hour to move

Tiffany's stuff back to suite 4F, but everyone, even Tiffany's old roommates, had pitched in. Lauren was right. Jeanine and the others did want Tiffany back, so Tiffany hadn't felt too bad.

"Let's hurry and get to the barn," Andie said. "I'm dying to find out more about last night's adventure." She stuck out her lip in a pretend pout. "I can't believe I missed it."

Mary Beth thought back to how scared she'd been last night. "Don't worry, you didn't miss much."

Grabbing their coats, Andie, Jina, Mary Beth, and Lauren raced up the hill to the stables. Mrs. Caufield was in her office with Dorothy. They were sitting around the desk drinking steaming mugs of coffee.

"Good news, girls!" Mrs. Caufield greeted them. "Thanks to Lauren, the police caught Mr. Previtti and his partner before they crossed into West Virginia with a truck full of tack."

"All right!" Turning to each other, the girls slapped palms.

"It seems those two are responsible for quite a bit of tack theft in the area," Dorothy said. "Since Pete delivered horses to a number of stables, he knew where everybody kept their equipment." She shook her head. "I've known the guy for years, too. Who would have suspected?"

"What did Pete do with the tack?" Mary Beth asked.

"He took it to an auction house in West Virginia," Mrs. Caufield explained. "He and his partner had quite a racket going, I'm afraid. But since they were caught with the stuff red-handed, they'll be in jail for quite some time."

"Will we get the saddles and bridles back?" Jina asked.

Mrs. Caufield nodded. "In a few days. And over the break, the school will install an alarm system for the tack room and office. We can't let this happen again."

"We were lucky this time, thanks to Lauren and Mary Beth here." Dorothy reached out and ruffled their hair.

"It's also lucky we're leaving for break today," Lauren chimed in. "Without tack, we wouldn't be able to ride."

"That's right!" Andie clapped a hand over her mouth. "I won't see Magic for a whole week!" She spun around and ran from the office, yelling, "I've got to give him a million kisses good-bye!"

After saying good-bye to the riding director and the stable manager, Jina, Lauren, and Mary Beth walked out into the aisle.

"I'm glad we don't have to say good-bye to each other yet," Mary Beth said, a lump forming in her throat. She'd suddenly realized how much she would miss Foxhall and her roommates.

"It won't be long before we see each other at Jina's." Lauren grinned excitedly. "I can't wait. A sleepover and a foxhunt!"

"I'm excited, too," Jina said. "And it's a good thing all this trouble at Foxhall is over, so we can concentrate on having fun at my house." She smiled shyly. "Well, I better go say good-bye to Superstar. My mom's coming to pick me up at noon, so this may be my only chance. See you two at breakfast."

After Jina left, Lauren turned to Mary Beth. "Hey, roomie, do you want to come with me to say good-bye to Fawn? I know you like her as much as I do," she added, ducking her head.

Mary Beth's stomach fluttered at the mention of Fawn's name. But then she grinned.

"Nope," she replied, pulling a carrot from her coat pocket. "I have someone else to say good-bye to. Dangerous Dan, my very own favorite horse."

And Mary Beth meant it.

Don't miss the next book
in the Riding Academy series:
#11: FOXHUNT!

"This is so much fun," Lauren said as she flopped down on Jina's canopy bed. "I'm so glad you invited us for a sleepover."

Jina sat down next to her, a bowl of popcorn in her lap. "I'm having fun, too. And just think, tomorrow's the foxhunt."

"What exactly is a foxhunt?" Mary Beth asked as she took a handful of popcorn.

Andie snorted. "What do you think it is, Finney? We gallop around on horses chasing a fox."

Mary Beth's hand froze halfway to her mouth. "But we don't really *catch* the fox, do we?" she asked hesitantly.

Andie leaned closer, a mischievous grin on her face. "*We* don't. But sometimes the hounds do. And when they catch it, don't look. It's really gross!"

"They kill the fox?" Mary Beth gasped, the popcorn falling from her hand. "Then forget about tomorrow. I'm not going!"

ALISON HART has been horse-crazy since she was five years old. Her first pony was a pinto named Ted.

"I rode Ted bareback because we didn't have a saddle small enough," she says.

Now Ms. Hart lives and writes in Mt. Sidney, Virginia, with her husband, two kids, two dogs, one cat, her horse, April, and another pinto pony named Marble. A former teacher, she spends much of her time visiting schools to talk to her many Riding Academy fans. And you guessed it—she's still horse-crazy!